DOUBLETAKE

Ana'Gia Wright

AZIZA PUBLISHING

DOUBLETAKE

An Aziza Publishing Book/ published by arrangement with the author
PRINTING HISTORY

Aziza Publishing Paperback Edition/ January 2014

For more information write to: Aziza Publishing
www.AzizaPublishing.com
ISBN: 978-0-9881767-8-2

The Aziza Publishing is a registered trademark.

PRINTED IN THE UNITED STATES OF AMERICA

Sheridan and Amira

Moving from one cabinet to another, Amira grabbed the nutmeg, cinnamon, and brown sugar from the pantry to add to the sweet potatoes on the stove. She added a few tablespoons of nutmeg and cinnamon and poured nearly half of the bag of sugar into the whipped potatoes blending the additional ingredients into a thick paste. She scooped a bit of it out, wrapping her lips around the spoon. A low umm escaped, her taste buds dancing with delight at the richness of the pie filling. Satisfied with the consistency of the mixture, she scooped spoonful's into the handmade piecrust and set them in the oven to bake and eventually brown.

Pouring the contents of the other pots and pans into individual containers, she placed the serving bowls and spoons in the middle of the neatly arranged plates and silverware. She filled two blue plastic cups and a sippy cup with orange juice for the children and poured wine for her husband and herself. Satisfied with the arrangement of the table Amira walked to the entryway of the kitchen.

Catching her husband's attention, she signed, *Can you get the kids? Dinner's ready.* When he stood up from the couch and walked towards the back hallway Amira turned her attention back to the empty space between the string beans and baked chicken. She headed toward the counter to grab the Mrs. Dash and black pepper.

The pitter-patter of little feet coming closer warmed Amira's heart. She loved her family so. A huge smile inched its way across her face as she watched her oldest son dash to the kitchen to plop down in his favorite seat next to his daddy's. Moments later Sheridan entered the cozy kitchen, their eighteen month-old son in one arm and their four-year-old daughter clinging to the fingers of his other hand.

He slid the youngest child into the high chair on the side of his chair opposite their oldest son before helping their daughter into her seat. Amira leaned back against the counter, her fingers wrapping around the edge. She stared at her husband as he held a silent conversation with their eldest son.

She still blamed herself for Nasir losing his hearing. He was completely deaf in the right ear and eighty percent hard of hearing in the left, all due to complications of the mumps. She still thought if she had kept his fever down her son would still have his hearing.

Warm fingers brushing against her cheek drew Amira from her thoughts. She hadn't realized that she'd spaced out. Her husband stood between her and the children not wanting Nasir to see their visual conversation.

*Are you ever going to stop bla*ming yourself, he signed, making sure she understood his question. They'd been through this before. He'd tried to convince her that sometimes these things happen. Nasir adjusted well to the loss of his hearing. He'd picked up sign language immediately, taking to it like it was second nature.

I know. It's not my fault, she signed back. *Still, he'll never hear the birds singing or even my voice anymore.*

He'll remember baby. Sheridan pulled his wife into a warm embrace rubbing his hand up and down her back. He understood how hard this was for her. Some days were better than others and this just happened to be a bad one.

Come on. The food is getting cold, and you need to feed that baby of yours. Sheridan intertwined his fingers with the rich dark chocolate ones of his wife, leading her to the table. He helped her into her chair joining in with the children in partaking in the wonderful meal prepared by the one he vowed to love forever.

They finished their meal in silence, the rules of the little game they played with the children still in effect. The days after Nasir first lost his hearing had been trying times for them. Everyone needed to adjust, and Sheridan had decided that the best way to adapt to their new situation was to make learning sign language a game.

It started out as just thirty minutes a day when they'd sit in the living room and try to hold a conversation completely in sign language. Then, as the weeks progressed, the thirty-minute sessions turned into hour-long sessions. By month's end, they'd been able to go six to eight hours without saying a word. Even their four-year-old daughter   picked up on the game.

Sheridan challenged each of his family members to try to go twenty-four hours   without speaking a word within their home. Amira usually lost, especially when Nasir's friends would come over. She'd end up fussing at one of them for tracking mud over her freshly mopped floor or drawing on her pristine white walls.

Nevertheless, this week started out quite well for the family. Not a word was spoken by anyone in nearly three days. If they made it through to the weekend, Sheridan promised to take everyone out for ice cream. Gathering up the remaining dishes while Sheridan helped Nasir with his homework, Amira stared out into the sunset just beyond the kitchen window. Her hands moved through the warm water, her fingers grabbing the rag to clean the butter from the pot she'd cooked the beans in. She inhaled the lingering aroma of freshly baked sweet potato pie, her tongue brushing across her bottom lip as she remembered the flavor from every single   rich bite.

As she placed the last dish in the drainer to dry, Amira dried her hands with the rag. Making her way across the living room, she picked up the pillows Sheridan had tossed onto the floor probably in some sort of ruff housing game with Nasir. She fluffed each one before lining it up on the couch with the others.

She found Sheridan with all the   kids in Nasir's room. He hovered over the smaller version of himself, pointing out something in the book while Nasir scribbled notes on the page. Their daughter rolled around on the floor with her baby brother playing tug of war with a stuffed bear nearly twice their sizes. Amira leaned against the doorframe watching the joy emanating from this one room in the house.

Sheridan didn't turn his eyes in her direction. She knew he'd felt her watching them so with a quick gesture, he signaled for her to take the other kids and get them ready for bed. This was their ritual. He'd comes home from a hard day's work of supervising over his construction business, take a relaxing shower and plop down in front of the television until dinner was ready. Then after dinner, he'd watch the kids and help Nasir with his homework while she cleaned the kitchen. Once she was done, she'd come keep watch over them for a few minutes until it was time to get the youngest of their children off to bed.

Scooping up their son and leading their daughter down the hall, Amira bathed, dressed and tucked each of the little ones in. By the time their daughter drifted off to sleep, and she snuck out of her room, Sheridan had already bathed Nasir. The two men, one old and the other on his venture of learning to become a man, stared at the toned ebony beauty smiling at them from the bedroom door.

She entered the room, taking a seat next to her husband on the chaise next to her son's bed. She pinched his cheeks, and he giggled at his mother. Amira took comfort in the light sounds her son released. Sometimes she forgot that he could still make sounds.

Ready for your bedtime story? Amira pulled a book of Native American legends from the shelf behind her husband. As she read the story from the book, Nasir's eyes remained fixated on his father's hands. Bedtime stories were the exception to the no talking rule. By the time they'd reached the fourth page in the story the little boy's eyes started to droop. At the end of the page, Sheridan placed a hand over his wife's indicating that their little one was fast asleep.

Closing the book, the couple tiptoed out of the bedroom and shut the door softly behind them. Amira turned, prepared to make her way to their bedroom to get ready for bed when Sheridan stopped her. Her eyes watched his hands as he signed, *you can talk you know?*

Why should I be the one to break the silence? I'd hate for the kids to lose their ice cream date with daddy. She eyed him, her hands placed firmly on her hips.

If I recall, you broke your silence last night. He made the famous air quotes before signing, *oh Sheridan, oh baby. That feels so good.*

Only after you whispered into my ear, she returned his imaginary quotation marks, *you like that? Tell daddy what you like.*

Amira walked away, leaving her husband with his mouth hanging open in the hallway. She hoped he didn't catch a fly in the gaping hole his mouth had become. She laughed to herself at the expression on Sheridan's face. He'd probably forgotten all about his little bedroom talk. She, however, had not.

Amira remembered everything about their lovemaking including all of the gentle caresses, the nibbling on her nose and collarbone and the way he traced her ears with his tongue. He always made sure to keep their sex life spicy. They'd watch flicks sometimes, she had a drawer full of toys, and some of the positions they'd tried; Amira had to stop thinking about it. Each thought made her hornier by the minute. Convinced her hubby needed some time to himself, Amira climbed into a warm relaxing bubble bath. She rested her head on the baby blue inflatable bath pillow as she sank back against the cool porcelain of their claw-foot tub. She inhaled, the scent of lavender, tea tree oil and vanilla soothing her mind. Taking care, she cleaned every crevice of her body as she washed away the tension of her day.

All clean, she climbed from the tub, sliding on her burgundy terry cloth bathrobe and matching slippers. Sheridan's mother gave her the set for their tenth anniversary. She'd had Amira's full name, Amira Jenay Malcolm, embroidered onto the right side of the robe. Sheridan had received one just like it, a perfectly match pair just like them. She sat on the bed for a while, reading while she waited for her husband to join her. After half an hour and no sign of Sheridan, Amira began to worry.

She searched the house; expecting to find him stretched out across the couch, remote in hand, sound asleep. But he wasn't there. She checked the kitchen thinking he'd gone in for a late night snack; no Sheridan there either. Sticking her head into the garage to make sure he hadn't left, she found his truck still in place.

Where could he be? Then it dawned on her, she'd looked everywhere but the one place she knew she'd find him. Sashaying her way through the kitchen door and back across the living room, she stopped in front of the closed study doors.

The past few weeks, Sheridan had been spending an increasing amount of time in the study. He usually retreated to the darkened room lined with rows and rows of books only when he had a lot on his mind. Amira had tried to get him to open up, but each time she asked if he was all right, he'd reply that he was fine, just had some things on his mind.

Tonight though, he'd been in there longer than any previous night and his behavior was getting more and more concerning. Amira wished he'd talk to her. They were partners in this. As his wife, she wanted to help him, be there for him, and aid him in sorting out any problems or issues he may have. The fact that he'd shut her out like this bothered her more than anything she'd ever experienced in the past. She couldn't fathom what might have her husband in such turmoil that he felt he couldn't come to her and talk about it.

Tapping on the hardwood of the door, Amira peeped

inside. The sound of Miles Davis floating through the air caused her heart to sink. She stared at her husband, the nearly empty glass of scotch on the table mocking her. She'd only seen him like this once before, when one of his closest friends had been killed in devastating plane crash. He'd sunk into a depression and she never wanted to see him like that again. And yet, here he was, that same look of despair, the blank stare, the sense of loss on his face and Amira was helpless to do anything for the man she loved.

She stepped into the room, pushing the door up so that the music didn't disturb the kids, and sat down next to her man. She placed her hand over his, just enough to get his attention.

"You want to talk about it?"

Sheridan continued to stare at the family portrait hanging above the light colored stone fireplace. He stood in the picture, the supporter of his family, with his wife by his side. Their three children, including the youngest that'd been only six months old when they'd had the sitting for the portrait, smiled back, happy, elated to be a part of this family. But Sheridan knew something they didn't know, something that could tear their perfect little world to shreds.

He'd considered telling Amira his secret, especially after the phone call from his mother, yet he hadn't been able to bring himself to do it. It wasn't the secret itself that would have the repercussions at this point. The truth was what it was. But the fact that he'd never told her something this important… Sheridan didn't know how Amira would take the fact that he'd hidden this tiny bit of information the entire length of their courting and marriage.

"No baby." He covered her hand with his other hand,

lowering his eyes in the process. "I know it's hard for you to see me like this but trust me, I need to handle this like a man."

Amira's sigh came from a place deep inside, a place that wanted to reach out and make things all better like a woman should be able to do when her man was in need. It was also a place that understood that a man needed to be a man and she'd have to accept that he wasn't ready to share whatever troubled his mind.

"Well, just know I'm here if you want to talk." Amira's lips brushed Sheridan's cheek, her reassurance that she was there for him when he needed her.

"Thanks." He finally turned to face her. "Try to get some sleep. I'll be in in a little while."

"Okay." She stood, her hand slipping away from the warm sandwich of his. "Good night."

Sheridan stared into those big round brown eyes of his best friend. They offered warmth, understanding, and companionship. So why was it so hard for him to reach out and accept the gifts?

"I love you," he confessed, knowing she saw doubt in his eyes. He tried to hide the questioning in his mind, but she'd always told him she could read his emotions; they were always plastered across his face.

"I love you too. Don't stay up too late." She made her way across the room, stopping at the door. With one last quick glance over her shoulder, Amira slipped out of the room, leaving Sheridan to deal with whatever issues he held in his heart.

Winston

Winston Malcolm stared at his computer screen watching the scores of black lettered C+ language scroll across the plaster of white. Adding line after line of code until the little scroll bar on the side of the page activated, he typed and typed away. His mind wasn't exactly on the program he was supposed to have finished by the end of this week. Instead, his mind drifted to the phone call from his mother, a phone call he knew sooner or later was destined to come.

Winston scanned the pile of CDs, zip disks, and paperwork that had become his shackles to this pitiful existence he called his life. True enough, his title as Lead Security Analyst afforded him a hefty six figure income which allowed him to travel on a whim to countries most people only saw in picture books or travel magazines it was still a hollow existence. He lived in a luxury home, the kind that could be compared to "The Hamptons." He drove a top-of-the-line Mercedes with a token Porsche for "special occasions" and even a motorcycle when he felt the need to become one with the open road, or more so test fate. He even had a special little lady who treated him like a king.

In that aspect, life was good. So why was he sitting here typing the name Sheridan Malcolm on the computer screen instead of the next line of code? Winston closed his eyes, running his hand over his baldhead, and then resting it on the back of his neck. If he looked as bad as he felt he could only be thankful for the fact that unlike most of the other bank technical staff, he had an office with a door.

Whipping his chair around to stare out at the downtown skyline, Winston pinched the bridge of his nose. Why did his mother have to call? He was doing just fine with his life the way it was. She just didn't get it. His brother had been out of his life for seventeen years now. As far as he was concerned, he didn't have a brother.

Winston leaned back in his chair, propping one leg on the opposite knee. He closed his eyes, focusing on fighting off an impending headache. He so didn't want to be here right now. If he could, he'd hop on his bike and hit the road with no particular destination in mind, just somewhere away from these four walls and any thoughts of his Sheridan.

Winston jumped at the sound of a woman clearing her throat. He was glad his chair was turned away. He didn't want to see anyone today and he knew exactly who the woman standing on the other side of the desk was.

"Just put the disk on my desk." Winston's attempt to keep the dryness out of his tone failed miserably. He dropped his head waiting for his boss's assistant to say something.

"What's wrong with you?" She waited for his reply refusing to be brushed off that easily.

He caught the curious look she gave him in the reflection of the window. She was probably wondering why he'd been hiding out in his office all morning when he normally would have made a couple of runs to the coffee shop by 11 A.M. The drumming of her fingers against the plastic case that held his disk of hacker programs for the day only made the pounding now pounding headache that much worse. What part of put the disk on the desk didn't she understand?

"I don't want to talk about this right now."

The woman turned and closed the door. She did however leave the blinds open. Their boss had walked past just as she'd entered Winston's office to deliver today's disk. She probably didn't want to arouse any suspicion by completely blocking out everything that could be going on in the office.

"You've been saying that for a week now. What's going on with you?" The woman cross her arms over her chest and glared at Winston.

Normally he wouldn't be able to see the gesture because he still hadn't turned around to look her in the face but every move she made was plastered in her reflection in the window. The cleaning lady must have gone ballistic with the Windex because Winston swore he'd never seen a reflection so clearly before.

"Didn't I just say I don't want to talk about it? Besides, work isn't exactly the best place for us to have this conversation." He swung back around, staring at the woman, waiting for her to try to deny the truth in his words.

They'd just seen two of their co-workers let go because

of a romantic relationship. True enough the woman was the young assistant's supervisor and under no circumstances did the other couple attempt to conceal their relationship. But the incident was too fresh in everyone's minds so they had to remain cautious. That meant keeping things strictly business while on the clock.

"Mark my words Winston Malcolm, this isn't over." She threw the disk onto the desk. Abruptly turning on one heel, she stormed toward and then out of the door.

Glad she didn't slam it shut behind her, he leaned back into the comfort of the leather executive chair. Door slamming in this usually quiet place would have drawn attention. He'd have to remind her tonight to keep her emotions under control, especially while they were at work.

Picking up the CD, Winston twirled the shiny silver circle on a finger. His mind again turned back to the brother he hadn't seen since high school. It wasn't like he didn't know what was going in Sheridan's life. Since he was the one who'd cut Sheridan off his mother never let a big event happen for Sheridan that she didn't call him about.

He knew when Sheridan and Amira got married, the birthdays of all of their children, and when Sheridan opened S&A Construction. She'd even called him when he'd gotten his first big contract. The list went on and on. It got to the point at one time where Winston just stopped answering the phone. Of course, that didn't last long. Winston loved his mother and father and inside he still loved his brother. But love and forgiveness were two different things and he still wasn't ready to forgive Sheridan for what he'd done.

Deciding that there was no way he'd be able to concentrate on work, he tossed the disc on the top of his to-do pile. He'd get to it, eventually. Instead, he clicked the little blue "e" on his desktop, and within seconds a new Internet Explorer window opened. He typed in S&A's web address into the search engine box and began his search to check up on his brother and his business.

Winston and Jasmine

S tepping from the shower in his home, Winston wrapped a towel around his waist. Though spacious, between the Jamaican Rum incense and hot water, his bathroom had become an aroma filled steam room. He stopped, standing in the middle of the floor inhaling the intoxicating bouquet. He loved the smell of the islands, one of the many reasons he frequented the Caribbean.

As he leaned against the shower door he fought to push his mother's words out of his head. Why wouldn't she just let this be? Why had she once again put herself smack dab in the middle of his life? Why couldn't she see that if he hadn't had anything to say to Sheridan in all of this time then there wasn't anything left to say?

Closing his eyes and sinking to the floor, Winston crossed his arms on his knees and laid his head there. So many thoughts raced through his mind. He did miss his brother; they used to be so close. Even when they fought, after one of them got the beat-down, they made up. But all of that changed in high school. Sheridan became the "favorite child." Sheridan made straight "A's." Sheridan made the football team. Sheridan this and Sheridan that.

"Winston? Can I come in?"

The timid female voice at the bathroom door pulled Winston from his moment of remembrance and self-pity. Instead of responding he pushed his way up from the floor and opened the door. He walked away from the brown skinned woman with grey eyes and straight black hair tied into a ponytail to keep it out of her face. He placed his palms flat on the sink counter using his weight to roll the tension from his shoulder blades. The last person he wanted to see right now was the slender woman standing behind him staring at his reflection in the mirror.

Turning his eyes up, Winston watched as she closed the distance between them. Her fingers massaged his shoulders as she leaned over to rest her chin in the bend of his neck. She titled her head to the side, darting her tongue in his ear.

"Don't." Winston shrugged her off.

"I figured by the time you got home you'd be over whatever has been bothering you. This shit is getting old Winston. You keep shutting me out and I'm going to be out." The woman stepped back giving him the space his expression clearly indicated he wanted.

"Then go. Nothing's stopping you." Short, simple, and to the point she'd brought it on herself. He'd told her that he didn't want to talk about it and yet she kept pushing. The crazy thing was he did want to talk about it. The "how" part was what he was still trying to figure out.

Her mouth dropped, her eyes glazing over. Not believing the words he just said to her, she walked out.

"Damn." Winston ducked out the door hoping to catch

his woman before she made it out of the house. He'd just upset her and the last thing he needed was for her to get behind the wheel or worse, walk the streets in her current state. "Jasmine!"

He found her in the spare bedroom, the bedroom she used to sleep in before they'd truly committed to each other. She'd curled into the fetal position on the bed. He watched her shake as she attempted to control the sadness. He'd caused her pain and he needed to fix this.

"Jasmine, I'm sorry."

"Whatever Winston. Just go away." She rolled over onto her stomach. Two could play that game. If he didn't want to be bothered, then she'd give him what he wanted.

"Listen," he reached for her and she slid away. "I deserve that. But hear me out. Please."

"Why should I listen now?" She wiped the tears from her eyes with the sleeve of her sweater. "I've been trying to get you to talk to me for weeks and all you've done is made me feel like shit."

"My mother called two weeks ago." Winston moved to the window. He pulled back the olive curtains and leaned on the windowsill.

"Is something wrong?" Concern replaced the anger and hurt. Winston's family meant a lot to him and if something was going on she wanted to help as much as possible.

"Not really anything wrong. She's pushing again, trying to get me to call Sheridan." This would be so much easier if he wasn't feeling like he should be trying to mend things with his brother.

"Winston, can I ask you something?" Jasmine stood, still keeping some distance between them.

"That all depends. You can ask but I can't say I'll have an answer." He still refused to look at her. He had a feeling about what she wanted to ask and maybe it was high time he told someone about that day.

"What happened? What could be so bad that it tore two brothers apart?"

She'd asked it, the one question that needed to be asked and answered. He thought about avoiding it, but the time had come for him to face the music. Their parents were getting older and he and his brother really did need to get this entire situation out in the open.

He joined his woman on the other side of the room, grabbing her by the hand. He led her into the master bedroom and pulled her into his arms as they relaxed against the mound of pillows at the headboard. Having her there in his arms gave him strength to relive all of the drama he'd been carrying around for all of these years.

"When we were little, me and Sheridan were tight. Let my mamma tell it, we were inseparable. But as we got older we grew apart. Don't get me wrong, we still had things we shared but it wasn't like when we were kids." Winston grew quiet. He missed wrestling with Sheridan. He missed just hanging out, playing pool, and driving around picking up women. Even though it had been seventeen years, the memories felt so fresh.

"Winston baby, you okay." Jasmine patted him on the hands. He'd withdrawn and it concerned her.

"Yeah."

"So, you two just grew apart?" Growing apart wasn't a convincing enough argument for brothers to be completely cut out of each other's lives. Something else had to have happened, he just needed to open up and tell her.

"That's where it started." Winston closed his eyes as he thought back to that day. He tensed, remembering what he'd seen. "In high school, we really became two different people. He was the jock and I was the hustler. He got A's and B's, I was lucky if I didn't have to go to summer school." He snickered, remembering the good old days before the shit hit the fan.

"I was the trouble maker and our father never let me forget it. They just didn't understand; I never wanted to really run the streets. Everybody thought I was this big time drug dealer just because I use to come to school in the latest kicks and the newest gear. They didn't know that I was just a small time number runner."

"Then why'd you let them keep believing it?" She shifted between his legs, getting in a more comfortable position.

"It was easier. I was finally my own person instead of just Sheridan's brother. I hated living in his shadow; Sheridan this and Sheridan that. The only good thing out of it was the honies, but not even a good lay could make me forget what he did."

Again Winston grew quiet. The anger started flooding back, threatening to spill over. He wasn't ready for this.

"What did he do baby?"

Winston squeezed Jasmine, holding her close to his heart. He wanted to tell her, the words fighting to escape the wall he'd erected around those memories. He couldn't do it though. Even after all of these years, it hurt too much to say it.

"He crossed the line; broke his word. And if a man's word is worth nothing, he's worth nothing."

"Winston…"

"I don't want to talk about this Jasmine. Just let it be. Okay?"

Jasmine wiggled her way out of his arms. She faced him, giving him her best bedroom eye impression. He looked so sad, so hurt. Whatever had happened all of those years ago, he still harbored. If she could get him to talk, maybe she could help. She knew though that Winston's stubbornness was a force to be reckoned with. She'd wear him down; eventually. Hopefully when he was ready to talk, he'd also be ready to make things right.

"Come here," she beckoned on hands and knees near the edge of the bed.

He raised an eyebrow at the seductive look she shot his way. He caught the hint. If he wasn't going to talk, then he was going to take care of her. Instead of going to her, Winston opened his arms waiting for her to come to him.

Moving like a lioness on the hunt, Jasmine crawled to her man. Nibbling on his nose, she moved down until her lips brushed against his. Tonight would be about him and she planned to make him forget all about his troubles until the sun again came up.

Amira

Amira scooped her youngest son into her arms and grabbed her daughter's daycare bag. Nasir, two steps behind his daddy, padded across the floor headed for the front door while Sheridan carried their baby girl. They'd finished breakfast half an hour earlier and Sheridan was on his way to drop the kids off on his way to work.

Following them out to the driveway, Amira propped the baby on her hip as she waved at her neighbors pulling out of their three-car garage. Squinting, she glanced up at the clear blue morning sky. Today was going to be a good day. After Sheridan left, she'd take the baby out to the guesthouse and hopefully get some work done.

Sheridan strapped their daughter into her car seat and Nasir climbed in next to her. After everyone was situated, he walked over to where Amira stood. He opened his arms wanting to hold and hug his baby boy before leaving them for the next few hours. The little boy giggled as his daddy made faces and tickled his belly.

"You gonna be good for mommy today?" Sheridan twirled them around knowing good and well that his son was too young to understand.

He stopped when the little boy started blowing spit bubbles, a sure sign he was going to spit up. "Watch out, he's going to blow." Sheridan handed the little boy to his wife and just as she laid him on the towel she'd tossed over her shoulder he spit up.

"See what you did. You know you shouldn't swing him around like that after he just ate." She wiped the little boy's mouth with a clean corner of the towel before hugging her husband. "Good luck with your meeting today."

"Thanks. I think this might be the big one babe. If I get this contract, once it's done I can cut back on my hours and help you out with the kids." His eyes lit up as he talked about the contract.

"Don't stress over it. I'm doing just fine, especially since you're taking that spoiled rotten one to daycare." Amira waved at her daughter through the tinted window of the vehicle.

"Hey. My baby girl is not spoiled rotten." He raised an eyebrow at her accusation.

"Um um um. That little monster has you wrapped around her little finger. She is definitely a daddy's girl. Go on now before you're late." Amira shooed her hubby away. He really did need to get going.

She watched as he pulled out of the driveway into the street. He waved good-bye as he pulled away from the curb. Amira turned around intending to get the baby cleaned up before she started work when someone called her name. Her head snapped around and a smile crept across her face as she realized her two best friends in the world were gawking at her from the bottom of the driveway.

"You done sent that man away Miss Amira?"

Amira rolled her eyes at the southern drawl of her good friend Madison Belflores. Sometime she wondered why she even stayed friends with the wench. "I didn't send him away. And aren't you two a little early?"

Mid-week the three women usually gathered together to talk about the happenings in each other's lives. The conversations about themselves only lasted about half an hour before Madison would start up with the neighborhood gossip. Wasn't much around here to do for the wives of the well to do except gossip.

Madison had only agreed to move into the upscale-gated community because of the breathtaking landscaping; otherwise she'd have been comfortable in her little high-rise loft downtown. Carmen, their third partner in crime, had been living in the same house since she'd married her CEO husband nearly twenty years ago. Amira and Sheridan had been in the community for eight years now and she loved every minute of it.

"Why, we just thought ya' could use some help." Madison replied, brushing a curl from her face.

Amira pursed her lips at the tan woman with the Shirley Temple locks pinned up in her golden hair. She would never understand how that woman spent hours in the tanning salon just to be brown.

"Come on," she gestured for them to follow her into the house, "let me get this one cleaned up and we can get started."

Stripping the spit and vomit soaked t-shirt from the

little boy; she wiped him down, slid on a clean navy blue cotton shirt and carried him back to the living room.

"Did you two really come here to help me or to gossip?" Amira shook a rattle in front of her baby boy and he wrapped his fingers around it, shaking it just like his mother had.

"I came to help. I don't know about Miss I just got my nails done here," Carmen, the down to earth CEO who married Mr. Where's my dinner, why you always working, are we ever going to have children said.

"I beg your pardon. I came to give the young lass a hand with her orders." Madison placed her hand on her hip, an understatement of the glare she shot at Carmen. "Not everybody can be the all-powerful queen of consulting."

"Enough you two." Amira nipped this in the bud. Those two would go after each other all day if she let them. "I have work to do. As for anyone who's willing to help, I'd greatly appreciate it."

Amira sashayed out the back door, strolling across the neatly manicured yard. Her husband had given his landscaping employees hefty Christmas bonuses last year and in return they'd come by the house and redesigned the entire back yard.

Where her rose bushes had once stood, they'd put a rock garden with a pond, a trellis and a wooden bench. Her rose bushes had been moved to the front of the guesthouse, lining the base as they wove their way through the attached white trellises. The men had moved the green house to the far corner where the rising sun could warm the plants and they'd laid out stone paths leading to each of the buildings or gardens. Even her berry bushes, apricot and peach trees had found new homes. To her surprise, the trees had made the transition without too much stress and given bountifully to them this year.

With her two friends close on her heels, Amira unlocked the guesthouse door and stepped inside. She'd come out earlier and opened the windows allowing the dew laced morning breeze to cool the interior.

The three women entered the two-bedroom one bath miniature home through the open area of the den. Sheridan had furnished the place like a miniature bachelor pad and sometimes he and the boys would come out to the guesthouse to watch games. Since all of the children were under ten, having drunken grown men spewing obscenities at all hours of the night wasn't exactly at the top of Amira's list. So, as long as they cleaned up after themselves, or Sheridan called in a cleaning service so Amira didn't have to do it, she had no qualms with them using the guesthouse for their rough housing.

Amira slid her baby into the swing perched snuggly in the corner of the kitchen between the counter and the bay window looking out over their backyard pond. She turned the metal contraption on, the gently rocking and soft music lulling her little one into a quiet slumber. She watched him for a few minutes, his facial expressions reminding her of Sheridan, as he drifted off to sleep.

All of their children looked just like him. They all had the same rich dark chocolate complexion and the cutest dimples. Their sons each had eyes a half a shade lighter than their father's and their daughter had gotten her mother's eyes, two endless dark brown pools.

Convinced that her little one was sound asleep, Amira opened the pantry door to pull out her four pre-made containers of soap and basket making supplies. Just like his father, her little one was a sound sleeper. Only the earth opening up at his feet, or tickling him under the chin, would disturb that boy.

"So how many do you need to get done today?" Carmen asked, grabbing six medium sized baskets from Amira's hands and placing them on the long white table in the middle of the floor.

"Two with a baby theme, one wedding themed, and four house warming gifts. There's a piece of paper stuck to the fridge with the color combinations." Amira stretched, attempting to reach the two large white baskets that slid further out of her grasps with each brush of her fingertips.

"Let me get that for you hun'." Madison, five inches taller than the five foot three Amira, reached with ease pulling the last two baskets from the back corner of the highest shelf. She handed them to Amira, "Here ya' go."

"I could have gotten them myself." Amira replied with a huff.

"Well I do declare I thought you asked for our help. If you don't think I can be of service, let me know now. I can always find sumtin' to occupy my time." Madison tooted her nose up in the air as she sauntered her way across the room to join Carmen at the table.

Something to occupy her time huh. Wonder if her husband knew that the gardener and the butler, not to mention the piano repairman have all been "occupying" her time. Amira was surprised Mr. Belflores hadn't caught on to the piano repairman. No piano was out of tune that much. But she kept her comments to herself. The last thing she wanted was to ruffle Ms. Prissy's feathers. Instead, she went

> **Comment [RL]:** Is this intentional or should this sentence begin with an "I"

about doing what she needed to do. She lined the soap molds up on the counter starting with the wedding molds and ending with the house warming ones. She placed the dyes and fragrance oils in front of their respective sets lining them up from the lightest color to the darkest.

Carmen and Madison busied themselves filling the bottom of the baskets first with newspaper then the corresponding tissue paper and coordinating filling. When the baskets were stuffed they joined Amira in front of the stove.

"Take the first two pots of the white soap and add three drops of color and ten drops of the fragrance. And make sure you stir while adding the ingredients, otherwise the soap will start to cool."

Madison sucked her teeth, not acknowledging the orders Amira spit out. It wasn't like they hadn't done this a million times before. "Whatever Madam Queen wants, Madame Queen gets."

"Maddie." Amira shot imaginary eye daggers at the woman. The abbreviated name alone was a clear indication she was treading on thin ice.

"Looks to me like someone isn't getting any." Madison continued her stride down the line of molds shaped like rattles and baby booties until she reached the sets with the hearts, doves and wedding rings.

"What is that supposed to mean?" Amira stopped stirring the soap to glare at the woman with the other pot in her hand. If Madison had wanted a reaction, she'd just gotten one.

"Mr. Tall, Dark and Handsome too tired from working

all those long hours to come home and take care of his woman. You know, my pastry chef can work wonders with those hands of his."

"Madison Belflores, are you suggesting I act like you and cheat on my husband?" Amira again stirred the soap keeping a film from forming at the top.

"I'm only suggesting you make sure your needs are met. If your husband can't meet them then…"

"Stop it Madison." Carmen had allowed this to go on for long enough. "Just because your husband turns a deaf ear to what you're doing doesn't mean that everyone in the world wants to live like you do."

"I beg your pardon?" Madison faced Carmen, not believing the words coming from the woman's mouth.

"You don't need to beg me for anything. You do enough begging to your man for all of us."

"Well, I never." Madison's eyes grew to the size of golf balls at the accusation.

"And you never will." Carmen added three additional drops of dye to the soap filled molds. As the heat warmed the cool liquid, it dispersed, leaving a tie-die pattern that would sink all the way through.

"All right ladies," Amira interjected, "enough of this bickering. We've all agreed that how Madison chooses to live her life is her business."

"Not when she's suggesting that you…"

"Carmen, let it go." Amira moved the top pot to a cool burner and placed the next one onto the boiling water of the double boiler.

They could go back and forth with this all day long and nothing would change. Amira had given up on convincing Madison that what she was doing was wrong. She'd never even entertained the thought of stepping out on Sheridan. She loved her husband and he was all she needed. He satisfied her just fine but she'd keep that to herself.

Amira finished a batch of clear soap, handing the pot off to Carmen to add the color and scent and pour it into the molds. They worked in the assembly line fashion until each of the molds held their respective colors and scents. By the time the last one was filled, Amira heard the whimpering of her son.

"Well ladies, shall we have our tea now?" She walked to the other side of the kitchen picking up her little one from the swing. It was time for his mid-day meal and the combination of all of the different scents was starting to irritate her nose.

They left the kitchen choosing to return to the main house instead of staying in the guesthouse. Amira prepared her little one's meal while Carmen placed the pastries on the tray and made the tea. As usual, Madison entered the kitchen and plopped down in the chair at the head of the table. She filed her nails and answered a few phone calls. She even excused herself to have a private conversation with no doubt one of her men on the side.

Amira didn't understand that woman sometimes. Madison and her husband slept in separate bedrooms, moved in different circles. How they ended up together was a mystery in itself and the fact that they'd been married for almost twenty years, Amira stopped trying to figure that one out a long time ago.

With the baby stretched across her legs, stuffed and fighting sleep Amira rocked him back and forth. She was glad he wasn't a really fussy baby. Some days, with that oldest one she'd feel like she wanted to tear her hair out. At least before he got sick.

"So," Carmen stirred a few drops of honey into her tea before continuing, "I haven't seen Sheridan that dressed up to go to work in a long time. You gonna tell us the scoop."

Amira took a sip of her tea, allowing the warm liquid to slide down her throat. "Not much to tell. He has a meeting today with some bigwig. Something about a contract."

"Must be a mighty important contract for him to have pulled out an Armani suit to go to a construction site." With her pinky held high just like her mama taught, her Madison took a sip from her tea.

Amira eyed the woman not taking too kindly to her scoping out Sheridan. She had to have been staring pretty hard for her to pin the suit as Armani and especially from the curb.

"Madison!" Carmen couldn't believe that woman.

"What?" She placed her teacup on the saucer and picked up a tea biscuit. "I'm only asking the obvious." She held her other hand beneath the pastry to catch any crumbs from her bite.

"You're being nosey," Carmen said.

"You call it nosey; I call it keeping well informed."

"Well for your information," Amira interrupted the exchange, "my business is just that, my business and I'd suggest you stay out of it."

"I think she means it this time Madison. You know she a crazy heifer."

Carmen knew for a fact that Madison didn't want to see that side of Amira come out. She'd seen it only one time before when some woman had tried to make a move on Sheridan. It wasn't a pretty picture. The woman moved two days later and the next thing they knew the gates at the bottom of the drive had been changed to read The Walkins.

"Point well taken. It was still a nice suit."

Though the latter half of her comment had been spoken under his breath, Amira still heard Madison's snide remark. She shot one last warning glare at the woman before changing the subject.

ANA'GIA WRIGHT

Sheridan

S heridan rolled to a stop in a parking spot in front of one of the many office buildings jutting up into the sky. Rows and rows of the black, white and gray buildings lined this street so much like the others in the business district. He'd dropped the kids off, checked on three of his eight jobs sites, making sure his foremen had all of the necessary supplies for the day. His assistant had called and confirmed that his meeting was still at one so he'd grabbed some lunch and made his way to the office building. He climbed from the vehicle, scanning the parking lot before walking in the direction of the door.

"Early as usual. You better be glad I know you otherwise your ass would have been sitting out here waiting for me."

Sheridan's head snapped around at the sound of the voice he recognized, the voice of his best friend, Terrence. "What makes you think you know me so well?"

"I know more about you than your wife does," the man teased shaking hands with Sheridan before giving his boy their secret handshake.

"Aye aye hold that down. That's why you can't tell folks shit."

"Whatever man." The two men entered the black glass front building and stepped onto the elevator.

"I appreciate you letting me use your office." Sheridan leaned against the mirrored walls, his eyes locked on the numbers lighting above the door.

"Hey, what's the point of owning a floor in an office building if you can't help your boys out every once in a while? Besides, it's nice to see a brother doing good for himself and his family. I wanna be just like you when I grow up." Terrence punched Sheridan in the arm.

"Yeah, *when* you grow up. I don't foresee that happening any time soon. Playboy."

"Call me what you like," Terrence flipped up the collar on his three-piece suit and adjusted the lapel. "I can't help it. The ladies love me."

"If you say so."

Terrence and Sheridan exited the elevator. Leaning over the counter picking up his mail from the inbox, Terrence left instructions with the receptionist that when Sheridan's guest arrived to buzz his office. In the meantime, they'd do a little catching up.

As usual Sheridan ignored the stares and sneers from the men and the women in the office. Terrance ran a small but profitable investment firm. His employees made good money for him, but that never stopped them from hating on others. Sheridan didn't use the office his friend offered very often, but this was a special occasion, one that could set him and Amira up for life, so he wanted everything to be on point.

"So," Terrance stretched his legs, propping his feet up on the desk, "must be some big deal for you to pull out a suit."

Sheridan sat across from his ling time friend, his attention placed on the city skyline just over Terrence's shoulder. He concentrated on keeping his hand from shaking. Why was he nervous? This deal was like any other deal.

"Sheridan!"

"Huh?" He blinked; must have been daydreaming. "What did you just say?"

"You starting to scare me man."

"I'm starting to scare myself." He ran his hand through the imaginary hair on his head.

"This guy must be talking top dollars to have the man with nerves of steel rattled." Terrence put his feet on the floor and propped his elbows on mahogany desk.

"This contract is worth some serious loot. Not only that, this is guaranteed work for my men for the next ten to fifteen years. I'm talking five states, multimillion-dollar complexes. I'm not doing this just for me and my family I'm doing it for all the guys who work for me. They deserve it." Sheridan leaned back in the chair locking his fingers behind his head.

"Then you know what you need to do. Don't worry about it. You got this."

Sheridan wished he were as confident as Terrence about the outcome of this meeting. He had some stiff competition. "I hope you're right. The other three companies up for this bid have been around for thirty plus years. I'm a feeder fish in an ocean of shark and piranha."

"This guy must have thought your company could handle this. Otherwise why would he be meeting with you?"

Before Sheridan could respond the phone rang.

Terrence pressed the intercom button on the phone, "Yes?"

"Mr. Harrington is here," the female voice replied over the speakerphone.

"Send him back." Terrance stood, relinquishing his seat to Sheridan. "I'll leave you two to talk business. Just let ole girl at the desk know when you're done."

Just as Terrence stepped through the door, a thin Caucasian man with red hair and freckles entered. The men locked eyes for only a moment before Terrence continued down the hall toward the front door.

"Sheridan Malcolm?"

"Yes sir." Sheridan extended his hand, offering a firm handshake. "You must be Mr. Harrington. It's nice to finally meet you face to face. Please, have a seat."

Sheridan closed the door. He said a silent prayer, hoping this meeting went off without a hitch. He took a seat across from this man and began their meeting.

#

Driving past a sign reading construction only entrance Sheridan made a right turn into the partially built strip mall. He pulled around a line of all American made pick-up trucks with his company logo plastered on the side and parked at the end of the row. They'd visited the two residential sites he'd check on before lunch and this was their last stop. Their meeting had gone well, or at least Sheridan thought it had and Mr. Harrington appeared to have been impressed by the two previous sites.

Sheridan watched from the corner of his eye as his potential client took in the surroundings. He was glad his client had allowed him to choose the sites. He had his top men working on this one. They had at least another six months before the project would be complete but they were almost two weeks ahead of schedule, news his client had been glad to hear.

Sheridan didn't know what to think. He tried not to stare, but he was trying to read this man. The man stood with his hands behind his back. His eyes perused the site taking in the orderly fashion in which the men unloaded the stacks of plywood from one of the trucks.

No longer comfortable with the silence, Sheridan asked, "Do you have any other questions?"

Mr. Harrington didn't respond immediately. Instead, he walked a little closer to the site. Sheridan was glad when the man stopped at the fence. Another step and he'd have had to ask him to put on a hard hat.

"No. I think I've seen all that I need to see." He faced Sheridan, "You've impressed me. Your men are extremely competent and they have drive. I like that in a contractor and his crew. And you; I must admit, I was initially hesitant about considering such a young company with such a young owner but I must say with your impeccable references and the way you've handled yourself today I have no doubt that your company could handle the jobs I have in mind. Can you free your schedule next week? I'd like for you to accompany me to look at a couple of out of state job sites for potential building."

Sheridan just stared at the man, not completely sure he understood. Or maybe his mind hadn't quite grasped the fact that it was possible that this man liked what he'd seen today.

"Mr. Malcolm, I'm offering your company the contract."

"Then my schedule is free next week." Sheridan slid a business card from his front suit jacket pocket and handed it to the man. "Just contact my assistant with the details." He again offered his hand to the man. "I do appreciate your business."

"I'm sure you do." Mr. Harrington walked past Sheridan. "There's my driver. I'll be in touch."

Sheridan stared wide-eyed as the man climbed into a Lincoln town car. As the cloud of dust dissipated and the rear of the car disappeared around the corner, he flipped open his phone. He dialed his home number still a little stunned.

"Sheridan! Sheridan baby, what's wrong?"

Sheridan looked down at the phone in his hand not realizing he'd turned the speakerphone on. He switched to the handset before responding, "Don't cook. We're going out tonight." There. He'd been able to get at least those few words out.

When Amira asked what the occasion was he replied, "We'll talk about it when I get there. Do you think your sister can watch the kids? I'd really like tonight to be just you and me." Sheridan headed back to his vehicle. He had one more stop to make before going home.

"Be ready by six. And wear something...nice." He thought for a moment, visualizing the one piece of clothing he wanted her to wear. "Think royalty."

Sheridan smiled at the sound of his wife's last words before the dial tone rang in his ear, *Umh. Royalty huh. I'll see you at six.* He knew she understood what he was getting at. She'd make sure her sister kept the kids so they could have a nice long private evening together.

ANA'GIA WRIGHT

Sheridan and Amira

"So I take it your meeting went well?" Amira ran the brush through her hair a few times more before she tied the end in a ponytail and wrapped it into a bun. She picked up her powder brush, brushing a thick layer of the dark substance over her face to neutralize the oil.

"In a manner of speaking, yes." Sheridan placed a crystal vase full of red and white roses on the vanity in front of his wife. Her smile lit up the room as she laid eyes on the spray of flowers.

He stood behind her, his hands resting on her bare shoulders, admiring his ebony beauty. She'd comprehended his little hint perfectly. The fit of the royal blue dress over her ample bosom did more to him than he cared to admit. And knowing that she wasn't wearing anything beneath the dress made this moment even that more torturous.

"Why are you looking at me like that?" Amira glanced at her husband in the mirror. If she didn't know any better, she'd have sworn he was undressing her with his eyes.

"I'd rather not say." He couldn't hide the lust in his tone. Seeing her like this made him want to grab ahold of her, toss her on the bed and make love to her.

She raised an eyebrow now having confirmation that he'd been doing exactly what she suspected. He'd get the chance to do that and more later.

"We'd better get going before we end up skipping dinner and getting right to dessert." He offered his hand to his wife, helping her up from her chair. He covered her shoulders with her wrap and with his fingers intertwined with hers he led her to the door.

Entering the kitchen, the couple stopped to say good night to their children. Even if dinner didn't last long, they'd be out long after the kids were in bed.

Sheridan signed to his son, *be good for Auntie Tara and help her with your brother and sister.*

I will. The little boy signed back his eyes lighting up at his father. *Goodnight mommy, goodnight daddy.*

Goodnight baby. They signed in unison.

Nasir went back to working on his homework while his parents and aunt held a conversation he could barely hear.

"You two have fun now. And don't worry about the little ones. They're in good hands." Tara bounced the baby on her knee while baby girl made a masterpiece for her parents with a blue crayon and a white piece of paper.

"You sure they're not going to be too much of a handful?"

Amira hated dumping the kids off on her sister under such short notice but she really wanted to find out what had happened at Sheridan's business meeting. He'd avoided the topic since he'd walked into the house. She wasn't sure how to take his silence but she hoped it was good news. Considering he was taking her out for dinner, the probability of good news was high.

"Go," Tara urged, wiping the drool from the little boy's chin, "Have fun and don't worry."

Amira opened her mouth, prepared to speak but her sister stopped her.

"Goodnight you two."

A moment more of hesitance, a glance or two at the children and Amira finally allowed Sheridan to usher her out of the house. He helped her into the vehicle before getting in the driver seat and starting it up.

"You ready?" He asked putting the truck in reverse.

"As ready as I'll ever be." Amira leaned over, pecking her husband on the cheek.

Sheridan pulled out into the street and headed toward the gate. Not even the sound of the radio interrupted the silence shared between husband and wife. Not an uncomfortable silence, a peaceful silence. The silence couples who'd been married for fifty years shared. The knowing and complacency of just being in each other's space, that's what Amira felt and he was more than sure Sheridan felt it as well.

Once in the corner booth of the quaint little West Indian restaurant, the couple ordered their meal. Amira took a sip of her ginger beer, holding her breath to keep the bubbles from burning her nose. Once the liquid slid down her throat and she was sure it was safe, she let the breath seep between the part in her lips.

"So," she placed the bottle on the table, staring up into her husband's loving eyes. "Are you going to tell me how your meeting went?"

Sheridan opened his hand to his wife and she slid hers into his. "There's some good news and there's some bad news. Which do you want first?" He kept his attention one hundred percent focused on the woman he'd vowed to share his life with. The longest they'd ever been apart was two days but this business deal would mean he'd be away at least a week and maybe longer.

"Give me good news first." Amira hid her apprehension. The fact that he had news at all was a plus. And since he had good news, the bad news couldn't be all that bad.

"The good news is, baby I got the contract." Sheridan smiled a little. It felt good to just be able to say it. And the joy in Amira's eyes only made the news that much better.

"That's wonderful! How much are we talking? Is there a time limit? How many sites…" She rattled off one question after another, not giving her husband a chance to get a word in edge wise.

"Whoa whoa whoa slow down baby. I think you need to hear the bad news before you go getting too excited."

"What could be that bad? You've got the contract. Do you know what this means for us and the people who work for the company?"

"Yes Amira," he raised his eyebrows, the worry lines in his forehead popping out into waves. He smiled at her, finally allowing some of his uneasiness to fade to the background. "This is going to mean so much too so many people. It's going to change so many lives, hopefully for the better. But it's going to change our lives too."

"Well I know that silly." Amira took in the concern on her man's face. It started to worry her. Maybe she had jumped the gun.

"Listen to me Amira, this job isn't just another contract. These projects are going to be stretched over a number of years." He took a breath, mentally preparing himself to give her the bad news, "And a number of states."

"What are you saying?" She tried to pull her hand back, but Sheridan's fingers tightened around them.

"The client asked me to clear my schedule next week. He wants me to go with him to check out some sites in other states."

"How long will you be gone?" It was Amira's turn to be uneasy.

"I don't know that yet. But I'm more that sure it will be at least a week. And this probably won't be the only time."

Amira tried again to pull her hand away, but Sheridan held on. She just stared at her husband, speechless. She knew how much this job meant to him, to the company, but she was in no way prepared to deal with her husband being gone for weeks at a time.

"Look," more than anything Sheridan wanted her to understand his predicament. He'd made a vow to her happiness and right now this was going to be a test for their marriage. "I know this is a lot to take in right now…"

"No it's not that." She raised her eyes, looking up at him. "This, this is… I don't know."

"If you don't want me to go I can ask…"

"No baby," Amira closed her eyes and smiled. He'd give up handling this deal personally for her and the thought warmed her heart. "You've worked long and hard over the years to make something like this happen. It wouldn't be fair to you…"

"This isn't just about me. You've stood by my side and supported me through the ups and downs with this business. I promised myself that I was doing this for us- you, the kids and me. I want you to know that I would never put anything before my family. And if it means walking away..."

"I'm okay with this Sheridan. I have my sister and you know Carmen and Madison will make sure I have everything I need."

"Are you sure?" She always amazed him. Whenever he found himself in a tight spot, she'd step out on faith and provide what he needed. That was one of the many things he loved about the woman sitting across from him.

"Yes baby I'm sure. I'm proud of you. And no matter what, I'm one hundred percent behind you on this."

Amira squeezed his hand, passing a sense of understanding and support to him. She loved Sheridan more than she'd ever loved any man. He was all she'd ever wanted and the fact that he'd walk away from something this big just to make sure his family was happy gave her the additional strength to believe that things would be just fine.

The couple waited for their food to be placed on the table before continuing their conversation. They each sat in silence for a few minutes, savoring the steaming, spicy food laid out before them.

Halfway done with his plate, Sheridan broke the lingering silence. "Terrance is going to come by in the mornings to pick up the kids and make sure they get to school. He'll swing by in the afternoons and drop them off and make sure you have anything you need."

"Sheridan…"

"Please baby. The kids need to keep their routine. And with you not having a license it's just easier for me to have Terrence do it. Besides, in case you haven't figured it out, I'm trying to compromise. I'd feel more comfortable with a man staying at the house…"

He'd thought about this long before this contract came about. He and Terrence agreed that if Sheridan ever needed to be gone for any length of time, he'd step in and make sure that Amira and the kids had what they needed. Terrence was the Godfather of all three of the Malcolm children and they'd spent enough time with him for them to see him as family and not a threat.

"You know how I feel about house guests." She cut him off, making sure he grasped her disapproval at his implication. "Even when Tara stays over, I have a hard time sleeping."

"That's why I'm just going to have him stop by. I figured we could do grocery shopping before I leave and if you need anything while I'm gone, you can just give him a call."

"I have friends of my own, ya know." She scooped another spoonful of rice and peas into her mouth, holding her smirk in check.

Sheridan didn't exactly approve of Amira's friends. Well, at least not of one in particular, Madison. He'd had to stop himself on a number of occasions from telling her husband of her extracurricular activities. Lately, Madison had begun to flaunt her affairs, showing up at Amira's monthly dinner parties with every man in her house but her husband.

Some days he'd come home to his wife sitting on the couch watching television with the phone next to her. He'd hear Madison going on and on about her escapades with one of her lovers, sometimes for hours. He'd cautioned Amira about that woman, but his wife was an adult so he'd let her decide when to deal with Madison and when to cut her off.

"You have *a* friend."

"Sheridan. Be nice. She just can't help it."

Sheridan almost rolled his eyes as she once again defended Madison. Lately, Amira found herself doing that more and more. It wasn't that she agreed with the woman; it was just that Madison was high maintenance in more ways than one. She'd gotten married only because that was what was expected of her. In many ways, Amira felt sorry for the woman.

"If she's not happy, why doesn't she just get divorced? It's not like she won't be taken care of. We both know that husband of hers will give her anything she wants whether they're married or not."

"She has to save face. Especially for her son."

Madison's son was as much a wreck as his mother. He spent so much time in rehab that his parents finally sent him to military school to protect the family name.

"That boy is going to grow up so confused, seeing his mother jump from bed to bed with God knows how many men. Does she even try to hide the fact that she's screwing around?"

"Not our business Sheridan." Amira narrowed her eyes at her husband. They'd been through this before and Madison was the last thing Amira wanted to talk about. They were supposed to be celebrating.

"So you say. Mark my words, that woman is trouble."

In actuality, Amira was starting to believe him. Lately she'd been keeping a close eye on Madison. Her friend had started drinking heavily and she wondered if she'd gone back to popping pills.

Some people just didn't know how to handle things. When she and Sheridan were struggling, Amira found peace through gardening and drawing or spending time with the kids. Cheating never crossed her mind. And popping pills? Never. The closest thing Amira ever came to popping pills were the sleeping pills her doctor gave her for her occasional bouts of insomnia.

"Sheridan, can I ask you something?" Amira might be opening up a can of something she wasn't sure she really wanted to open, but she'd suppressed the inkling for some months now. Trusting her husband was one thing. Something told her that she should heed his advice and keep a closer watch on Madison, especially now that she'd been paying closer attention to some of the woman's comments.

"I'm an open book." He shot her a curious glance over the rim of his glass of iced tea.

Sheridan gave her a few minutes to gather her thoughts. He watched as a plethora of emotions danced across her face. They ranged from apprehension to sorrow. For an instant he even thought he saw regret.

"Amira? What do you want to ask me?"

She released a heavy sigh, realizing that she'd already started this so she might as well finish it. "I want the truth."

He stared at her, wondering why she'd started off with that. "Haven't I always told the truth? What's this about Amira?"

"Madison," here goes nothing, "has she ever approached you? I mean like propositioned you?"

"Where is this coming from? Just a minute ago you were defending her." His eyes narrowed, the waves in his forehead bulging.

"She said something earlier that sort of got under my skin. Any other time I'd have ignored her comments but for some reason it's been on my mind since this morning."

"What did she say to you Amira?" Sheridan dropped his fork, devoting his utter attention on his wife. He'd overlooked a lot of things that Madison said over the years. The woman was who she was. But upsetting Amira was a whole 'nother issue.

"Well you know how nosey she is? She asked about why you were so dressed up today." Amira stopped there again having second thoughts about continuing this conversation.

"And?" Sheridan continued to focus on her. His food was getting cold but that didn't matter. If Madison had crossed the line, he'd handle her himself.

"She made it very clear that she's been scoping you out."

He leaned back in his chair, crossing his arms before replying, "And how is that?"

"I know she didn't get a good look at what you were wearing. Even from the distance between the street and sidewalk, she couldn't have gotten that good of a look. And yet, she knew your suit was Armani."

"Lucky guess?" he asked, trying himself to figure out how she knew the suit was Armani.

"Not with Madison. Nothing is a lucky guess."

"So how do you think she knew?"

Amira lowered her head, not wanting him to see the accusation in her eyes. Though he'd never given her any indication that he'd stepped out on her, Madison's comment had ignited a sense of doubt of his sincerity. And with him about to be out of town for a week or more, she was feeling more insecure than ever.

"Amira, look at me." Sheridan waited but when it became painfully obvious that she wasn't going to adhere to his request, he slid a finger beneath her chin and raised it. "You do know that you mean the world to me, don't you?"

"Yeah, but she's Madison. With the bat of an eye she could have any man out there."

"Not this man. Not now, nor have I ever entertained the thought of doing anything that would jeopardize what we have. You are all I need. You're all I've ever needed. Don't ever doubt that. You understand me?"

"Yes." Her reply came across timid. She still had her doubts but he'd reassured her some that he felt she could provide anything he needed.

"And to answer your question, she's never formally approached me though I nipped those wandering eyes of her in the bud the first time she thought to wink at me."

"I'm sorry."

"There's nothing to be sorry about. I'm just glad you felt you could come to me with this. I love you Amira, and nothing will ever change that." Sheridan leaned over the table and brushed his lips against hers. He understood her uncertainty and he'd do what he could to comfort her and make her believe that he'd always be faithful.

Winston and Jasmine

J asmine rolled over in bed, expecting Winston to be resting comfortably beside her. Instead she found empty cold sheets. He'd been gone for a little while for his body heat to be gone. She felt the warmth from the heated bed but Winston's body temperature always made the bed feel like it was on fire. She liked the warmth his body offered, especially on cold winter nights when snow covered the world just beyond their window.

Securing the belt of her robe around her waist, she slid on a pair of flip-flops. He'd closed the bedroom door to keep from disturbing her. Sometimes he was so thoughtful. She stuck her head out into the hallway and listened. She followed the sound of the Isley Brothers past the other bedroom until she stopped in front of their office. Peeping around the corner, she watched the flickering of the computer screen on the picture of Tupac hung on the wall.

Apparently he hadn't noticed her so she decided to go make them some coffee. Maybe convincing him to talk in the middle of the night would pan out with better results. He was usually more open to talking after she gave him some.

As quietly as possible, Jasmine brewed two cups of coffee adding sugar to both of the cups and cream to hers. She carried the two mugs out of the kitchen and headed back towards the office.

"Hey," she said entering the dimly lit room. Jasmine hated when Winston sat in the office with all of the lights off staring at the computer screen. She'd told him time and time again it was bad for his eyes. Needless to say, he continued to ignore her.

Winston glanced over the top of the monitor at the woman he'd left sleeping soundly in their bed. He almost made a comment about her unruly hair. Then he thought better of it. It was his fault that it looked like that.

"I didn't wake you, did I?" He asked rubbing his goatee.

"No. Thought you could use some coffee." Handing him his cup, she kissed him on the cheek. She slid the swivel chair from behind the other desk and rolled it up next to him.

"What are you doing?" She kept her attention focused on him, not sure if he wanted her to see what was on the screen.

Jasmine tried to allow Winston to take the lead in most of their discussions. It was his decision if he wanted to reveal what he was up to. She'd learned early on in their relationship that directly pushing only made him shut down. When he was ready to talk he was ready to talk but when he wasn't pushing only made things worse.

"Looking for a flight." He typed in another site trying to find the best deal under such short notice. He hadn't thought too far ahead in this. He wasn't really sure he'd be able to go through with it.

"Going on a trip?" She twirled around in the chair staring at the ceiling.

"You might say that. You kinda got me to thinking." His gaze remained fixed on the computer screen. He knew where this was going. She'd asked him the same question she asked earlier but this time, he'd give her an answer.

"You ready to tell me what really tore you and your brother apart?"

Winston chose a flight and entered his credit card number. He waited for the confirmation and when the little yellow envelope popped up on the bottom right corner of the screen indicating he had a new email, he closed the browser window. He grabbed his cup of coffee, taking a sip before turning around to face Jasmine.

He glanced around the room, his gaze resting momentarily on the picture hung above the mantle before his eyes locked with hers. "Me and Sheridan use to be prime catches in our hey-day. I don't even remember half of the girls I hooked up with. Some of them I got with before Sheridan, some after. Even got with a couple when they were together. He always knew though; I made sure of that. And as long as he was cool with it, wasn't no problem. The same went for me, as long as we didn't get any surprises, no harm no foul."

"You two used to switch girlfriends?" Jasmine gave her man a disapproving look. She wondered how many of those women knew about this little game.

"Hey, the chicks didn't mind so why should we. There were a few who were off limits and we both respected that line. Or at least I did." Winston again retreated to that place in his mind where he went to avoid the day he'd walked out of his brother's life for good.

"Winston, what happened?" Jasmine understood how hard this was. They'd never talked about what happened between him and his brother. The longer she listened to his silence, the more assured she became that he hadn't told anyone else about that day either.

"Stupid me. I fell in love. We had the off limits discussion about the girl and I thought he was cool with it but I walked in on them hugged up on the couch one day. I didn't even say anything, I just left."

Jasmine covered Winston's hand with hers. She leaned over so that she could look him in the eyes. "So you never talked to him about what happened?"

"What was the point?" Winston snatched his hand way. "I saw all I needed to see. I even skipped out on graduation so I wouldn't have to see him or her."

"Oh Winston, I am so sorry."

"Don't be. I figured by now he'd try to find me to at least apologize. Apparently a relationship with his brother has been the last thing on Sheridan's mind."

Jasmine reached out to him again and this time he allowed her to intertwine her fingers with his. She'd sensed a bit of jealousy in his reply. They'd talk about that later. He'd taken an important first step acknowledging, accepting and talking about the major event that altered his relationship with his brother. She suspected there was more to the situation than what Winston thought he saw. She'd work on convincing him to take the initiative some other time.

Not wanting him to have to relive all of the memories at once, Jasmine moved the conversation in a slightly different direction. "What did your folks think about you just up and moving out like that?"

"My dad was glad I was gone. He didn't exactly agree with the crowd that I hung with. He said they were a bad influence on me. Guess he didn't realize by my senior year, I was the bad influence."

"And what about your mom?" She took another sip from her mug, turning at the first signs of sunrise outside the window.

"Mama just wanted us to all get along. Of course that was never gonna happen. Wasn't no reason for me to hang around. They had their favorite child so I bounce."

"Where'd you go? How'd you survive?" She faced him, sliding in closer. She almost reached out to hug him. She wanted to support him, help him get through this. She'd leave it up to him though to decide the next moment of physical contact.

"The night I walked in on them I packed my shit and moved in with one of my boys. I hustled for a while, watched a few of my peeps get put six feet under. Spent more time in a court house than most lawyers." Winston laid his head on the back of the leather chair. He allowed his mind to wander, thinking of the day he'd decided to change his life.

"So how'd you end up here?"

"The game got to be old. You get tired of watching your back after a while. Then, one of my partner's little boy got killed; caught in the crossfire over some bullshit ass drug deal gone bad. Seeing that little boy drop… I tried to save him," Winston grabbed and rolled his shoulder. He'd caught a bullet in the arm trying to save that little boy. "I was too late." He looked down at his hands, the blood of that little boy still fresh on them.

No longer able to keep the narrow distance between them, Jasmine draped an arm over his shoulder. He winced at her touch. Startled, he considered pulling away, her touch distracting and yet comforting. He pulled the woman who wanted to help him so much into his arms instead, coaxing her to come sit on his lap. He held on to her. She was real. She was here. The rest of that stuff was just memories.

"You want to hear what I think about all of this?" Jasmine swung her legs over the arm of the chair and wrapped her arms around her man's shoulders.

"What?" He raised an eyebrow, the glow from the computer screen casting an eerie shadow across her face.

"I think you've turned your life around. I think you've come a long way from being that little boy who was his brother's shadow. I think you've worked hard, sacrificed, and made something of yourself. And I'm proud of you."

"Thanks." At least somebody was.

"I also think you're a bigger man than this. You should really consider taking the first step. What happened between you and your brother was tragic no doubt but I think you owe it to yourself to find out if there was anything more to what you saw."

There had to be more to the story. Winston's clear-cut explanation just didn't add up. Seeing his brother hugged up with his girlfriend without any explanation for all of these years didn't sit right with her.

"And why should I?" Winston pushed her away. Lucky Jasmine knew her man so she'd prepared for the reaction. She stumbled a little before gaining enough footing to sit in the chair she vacated. "He should be the one to make the first move."

"Come on Winston. Think about this, what's the first thing you do when you get pissed?" Winston quieted down, searching his memory for whatever it was she was trying to get at.

"How about I help you out? You cut the phones off. You delete voicemail messages without listening to them. Any of this ringing a bell?" She leaned over to look him in the eyes, making sure he paid close attention, "You change the caller id to read do not answer."

"So." Pushing the chair away as he stood, Winston made his way over to the window.

"So? So, who's to say Sheridan didn't try to reach you? Who's to say he didn't call trying to explain. When you've cut somebody off, you cut them off. Even if they wanted to find you, you'd make every effort to avoid them. You hold grudges Winston and not everyone can wait for you to decide you're ready to talk to move on with their lives."

"Are you trying to say this is my fault?" He glared at her, not believing what she was saying to him

"Not at all. I'm just saying it's been a long time. You two need to work this out. It doesn't matter who takes the first step; somebody needs to do it. Reach out to him Winston. Your brother just might surprise you."

She joined him in front of the picture view of the rat race below. She kissed him, stopping the words about to escape. She'd planted the seed hoping he'd take her suggestion to heart.

"I'm going back to bed." Jasmine left Winston to think about what she'd said. Little did she know; he'd already begun planning a trip to visit his long lost brother.

Winston

Winston sat on the edge of the bed staring down at his honey beauty. He'd met Jasmine the day he'd been promoted from a low life programmer to lead security analyst. Other than the fact that his new job allowed him to do what most people considered illegal, she'd been the only other perk of the promotion.

The first day he saw her he'd felt an immediate attraction. He couldn't keep his eyes off of those legs that went on for days. He remembered licking his lips as she sashayed past his office door. She'd been wearing a blue and white floral dress that stopped just above her knees. The material swayed with each step. He knew then that she was destined to be his.

Their relationship started off strictly platonic. She was the boss's assistant so Winston decided to get a feel for her before asking her out. The last thing he needed in a new job was to ruffle anyone's feathers.

Every morning Jasmine went out of her way to make sure he got fresh coffee. She even started stopping by when she headed out to get lunch just to make sure he didn't want her to pick him up anything. The stopping by eventually turned to lunch dates and the next thing Winston knew, he'd asked to see her outside of work.

They'd decided early on to keep whatever this was evolving into on the hush hush. Although she didn't work for him, they worked in the same corner of the office. They were adults capable of having a relationship without bringing drama into work and surprisingly so far, outside of an emotional day or two, the situation panned out well.

"What's on your mind?"

So absorbed in his thoughts that he hadn't realized that Jasmine was awake, he stared down into those mysterious eyes of hers. "You."

"Really?" She blew a kiss at him, running a hand up his arm.

"Yeah. You know, it's not fair that you get the day off and I have to go to work."

She wrapped her fingers around his tie, pulling him to within inches of her lips. "You can always call in sick." Just as the last whisper of words escaped her lips, she planted a soft wet kiss on his.

Winston slipped his tongue between her parted lips, savoring the warmth passing from her to him. He encircled her waist, pulling her from beneath the sheets to straddle him on the bed. Realizing if they continued like this he'd never get to work he drew back, ending the string of passion between them.

"I have work that needs to get done. But how about this, I'll try to sneak out a little early and we can finish this then?" Winston gave her a devilish grin.

In return for his seductive smirk, Jasmine kissed the tip of his nose, his chin, his cheek and eventually darted her tongue in his ear. "You want anything in particular for dinner?" She whispered, her warm breath tickling the hairs on the back of his neck.

"I can't think about dinner right now. Dessert's looking a little too good."

Jasmine slid off of his lap and crawled back into bed. "The sooner you get to work, the sooner you get dessert."

Winston took the hint. Getting up from the bed, he kissed her once more before heading out the door. He'd warned her about asking for trouble and with the look she'd shot his way, tonight she'd get a lesson in trouble she wouldn't soon forget.

***

Cell phone in hand, Winston walked back and forth across the space behind his office chair and his computer desk. Jasmine was right. He should have just called in sick. He'd been in the office nearly three hours and hadn't so much as slid a disk into the computer.

This entire situation was starting to overwhelm him. His mind was racing. Was he really ready to do this? Would Sheridan be happy to see him? Had he even told his wife he had a brother?

The questions haunted every moment of his drive to work and every minute he spent confined to the walls in his office. He'd picked up the phone a couple of times calling Jasmine just to bounce some ideas off of her. This time though he called the one woman he knew desired to hear what he needed to say. He almost hung up the phone when he realized his father had answered instead of his mother.

"May I speak to Mrs. Malcolm?" He hoped his father hadn't recognized his voice. His parents didn't have caller id. As a matter of fact, as far as he knew they still had rotary phones.

He'd meant what he'd told Jasmine. Since leaving that house, he'd never returned. He hated arguing with his father and his mother's constant ranting about Sheridan was enough to keep him the fifteen hundred miles away from them. He needed to talk to her now though, and if there was one thing that his mother always wanted to talk about, it was Sheridan.

Winston cringed as the male voice on the other end asked who was calling. Not able to come up with a name off the top of his head he told the truth, "It's Winston."

He waited for a reply, some smug remark, anything. All he got was the crashing of the phone, probably on the marble counter of their newly remodeled kitchen, and the sound of his father yelling to his mother that "her" son was on the phone.

The hair on his arms stood on end as his anger escalated. He listened as his parents argued. One day he and his father were going to have it out about the way he talked to his mother. He hated it when the man took out his anger on the innocent woman.

And of course, the first words out of the woman's mouth were what's wrong. "Nothing's wrong ma. I just needed to talk to you about something."

He listened as she dragged one of the stools from the

island over to the counter so that she could sit down while he spilled his guts. For some reason, he believed his mother had known he was going to call. Now that he thought about it, she probably did. He wondered if she'd even talked to Jasmine. Maybe that's where all of the questions had been coming from.

The soft spoken woman on the other end calling his name jarred Winston out of his momentary slip into that crazy place in his mind where he went to contemplate how screwed up his life was.

"I called to ask about Sheridan." He expected her to be surprised, taken aback even. Instead she asked him one simple question.

"Yeah," he replied, "I'm thinking about going to see him. I even bought a plane ticket last night."

Winston walked to the other side of the office and closed the door. He closed the blinds as well. This was a private, personal conversation. No one would barge in with the blinds closed. They'd at least knock first; giving him the opportunity to put his mother on hold to take care of whatever emergency might arise.

"No ma. I haven't talked to him yet. Look, I'm at work and I can't talk long. I just have a question for you."

He sat in the chair, turning it to face the window as his mother went on and on about how he didn't call enough and now that he was calling, he was rushing her off of the phone. When she finally quieted down enough for him to get a word in edge wise, he blurted out the question. "Did Sheridan ever tell you why I left?"

The line grew quiet, too quiet; the kind of quiet you

hear in a mortuary. Winston held his breath, the anticipation draining him. Had Jasmine been right? All of these years, was there something he'd missed?

"Ma?"

She danced around the answer for a few minutes, telling him the story for the fifty millionth time about the day she'd discovered that he and his brother had been seeing the same girl. They kept their little "game", if you will, to themselves, making sure to avoid the house at all cost. They never figured out how she found out but when she had, she'd cursed them both out seven ways to Sunday about the situation. She'd warned them that sooner or later their little "game" would catch up with them. And she was right.

"Yes or no ma? Did he tell you?"

His mother usually gave straight answers and that's what he'd called her for, a straight answer. Unfortunately the only answer she gave was if he wanted to know, he needed to call his brother himself.

"But ma…" She cut off his whining before he got started. "Well, let me go then so I can call him."

She perked up at the mention of him calling Sheridan. She assured him that she was doing this for his own good. Grown men shouldn't have their mothers in the middle of their business. And yet, she'd always found a way to put herself in that spot.

Winston stared at the phone for who knows how long, the numbers and light on the screen mocking him. He'd picked it up a couple of times glancing over at the number his mother had given him for Sheridan. Something inside kept him from calling. Truth was something inside kept yelling that he was fooling himself. He wasn't ready to face Sheridan. Or maybe he wasn't ready to face the possibility of reliving what his brother had done to him.

One phone call wasted, Winston went back to doing the one thing he was good at. Work was the last thing on his mind but that didn't mean that the computer sitting on his desk would lay dormant. Over the years their mother had given him glimpses into his brother's life. Outside of his family though, she hadn't said much about Sheridan's life.

Winston knew his brother owned a construction company and knowing Sheridan, he'd have put his all into making it a success. He decided to surf the Internet to see what he came across. Typing S&A Construction into the search engine, he read headline after headline.

S&A Construction, investment in the future. S&A Construction gets award for minority small business of the year, S&A construction lands multimillion dollar deal.

The last headline caught Winston's attention. Multimillion dollar deal huh? His eyes widened at the sight of the big bold letters across his screen. He clicked on the link, reading the information provided in the article. Seemed his brother had done quite well for himself. He scanned further into the article taking in the span of the project. Sheridan would be set for life once this deal was done, another case of things falling into place for Mr. Goody-two-shoes while the rest of the world had to work for a living. Not that Winston had expected otherwise.

He so hated how easy things came for Sheridan. While he had to study twice as hard to make a C, Sheridan sailed through school spending most of his time with the ladies.

Though they both had women attracted to them, for some reason he usually ended up with his brother's leftovers. And outside of hustling and stealing, Sheridan beat him at everything: sports, video games, even dressing. He just couldn't catch a break.

Winston grabbed the phone, dialing the number of a good friend. Everybody with a public life had dirt. He just needed to find out what Sheridan's was. He hadn't figured out how he was going to use the information, but it would come to him sooner or later.

Amira and Tara

Becoming more and more disgusted with the person at the door ringing the bell like a five year old on Halloween, Amira secured the diaper on her youngest child. With her son on her hip and her daughter following on her heels, she made her way out of the nursery toward the door.

"I'm coming! Hold your horses!" She peeped around the curtains covering the narrow window to the right of the door. She shook her head when she realized the guilty party was none other than her sister.

Amira turned the key in the lock and the little gold knob on the doorknob to let her sister in. "Left your key again?"

"What took you so long? And why didn't you answer the phone? You had me worried." She stepped across the threshold, picking up her niece and twirling the little girl around. The squirming dark brown skinned child giggled with delight as the world became one big blur.

"I was changing the baby. And if you were so worried, why didn't you use the key hidden under the flowerpot?"

Amira left her sister at the door making her way to the living room.

"I didn't even think about that. So what's up? Where's Sheridan?" Tara closed the door and followed her sister.

Amira put the baby into the playpen. She placed a cardboard puzzle and ten unique shaped pieces on the floor in front of her daughter watching as the little girl tried to piece together the image of a dog chasing after a cat. She sat on the couch across from her sister.

"Out handling business. Guess what?"

Tara gave her sister a curious look. Excitement was one emotion she rarely saw in Amira. Even when Sheridan proposed, she showed happiness, even a tad bit of elation, but she made sure not to show excitement.

"Okay, spill it."

"Sheridan got the contract."

Tara jumped from her seat, plopping down on the couch next to Amira. She wrapped her arms around her sister, "When did you find out? Why didn't you call me?"

"Slow down, slow down. He found out Tuesday. I've been meaning to call but I've had loads of stuff to do."

"Stuff like what Mrs. Housewife?" Tara narrowed her eyes at her sister. How dare she keep this to herself?

"Well there was bad news that came with the good." Amira reached down sliding the correct piece to her daughter to place in the center of the puzzle.

"What kind of bad news?"

"The client asked if Sheridan could go with him to check out some sites so it's going to be just me and the kids next week."

"Oh." Sadness bled into Amira's eyes. Tara hated to see her sister like this. "You want me to come stay? I've got some time at work I can take."

"No. I'll be fine. Sheridan's going to have Terrence stop by to take the kids to school and bring them home."

"And what about you? I know this will be the first time that you two will be apart for more than a day or so?"

Tara allowed her concerned for her sister's well-being show. Amira had never really been alone. They'd shared a dorm room their first year of college and she'd gotten married their second year and moved in with Sheridan. Nasir had been born a few years later so when things got hectic for Amira, Tara always made sure to come by and check on them.

"Yeah, I guess I'm okay with it."

"Guess? Spill it Amira."

"Look, if I tell you this, you have to swear you won't say anything to Sheridan." Amira leaned down to get a little closer to her sister. Though her daughter was only four, she was old enough to repeat some words. Words she didn't want Sheridan to hear.

"What's wrong?"

"Swear." She waited for Tara to say the word before revealing what was on her mind.

"Fine. I swear."

"Well, for the last few weeks something has been going on with Sheridan. He's been spending a lot of time by himself. And last week I even had to coerce him into sex. I don't know what it is and he doesn't want to talk about it."

"You sure it's not stress. I mean if he's known about this contract for a while, maybe he's been worried about the outcome."

"That could be," Amira's head snapped around as her daughter released a squeal. She smiled as the little girl clapped her hands delighted that she'd been able to get the puzzle properly put together. "But I think it's something else. This has been going on for some time now. Way before this contract. I tried to get him to talk about it but he just keeps shutting me out."

"Amira, don't go pushing now. Sheridan is a strong man. Let him deal with this on his own. When he's ready to talk, he'll come to you."

"I keep telling myself that but don't you think this is a little convenient? He starts to withdraw, doesn't want to have sex and now he gets a job that is going to be taking him away for weeks at a time."

"No Amira, I don't. That man loves you. He'd do anything for you and the kids. But sometimes people need some space. You two are both maturing. You're reaching a new milestone in life and that takes some adjustment. There's no telling what that man has on his mind."

"You know I don't like being shut out." Amira kept a close eye on her toddler as the little girl started to inch her way to the other side of the room, probably in search of her older brother.

"Let this be Amira." Tara placed her hand on her sister's leg.

"I'll try. I just keep thinking that there might be something he's not getting from me and I don't want..."

"Stop it. Stop it right now. That man is not now nor will he ever be cheating."

Tara glared at her sister. She needed to get any thoughts of her man not being happy with her out of her head, especially now that Sheridan was going to be gone for a week. The last thing she needed to have on her mind was him with another woman.

"Fine. I'll let this go. But I also think there's something going on with his family."

"Like what?" Tara peered over her shoulder at a sound from the playpen. She watched her nephew roll over before he went back to sleep.

"He's been on the phone with his mother a lot lately. Every time I ask if everything is okay, he says everyone is fine. She calls once a week now and usually only talks to him."

"You think maybe she's sick?" Tara's concern escalated. She knew how close Sheridan was to his family and if something was going on with them, it could be the cause of his shutting out her sister.

"I don't know. I don't know what to think anymore?" Amira's shoulder slumped as the weight of not knowing sunk down on her. She didn't know how much more of this she could take.

"Look," Tara gave her sister a hug, "Give him some

time. Talk to him. Let him know that you're here for him if he needs you. But don't crowd him and don't push. He'll come around. You'll see."

Amira glanced over at her daughter, the female version of her husband. She was so young, so carefree and she didn't want anything to jeopardize her chances of having a good life.

"I pray you're right Tara. I pray you're right."

Amira stood and peeped over into the playpen to see her infant sleeping. They were so fragile, so needing, and so precious. And yet she felt just as vulnerable as they looked. She'd never do anything to break up her family and she just needed to have faith that Sheridan felt the same way.

Winston

Winston dialed the number of his friend, trying to find out what kind of information he'd been able to come up with about Sheridan. The last time they'd talked, he was camped outside of Sheridan's home trying to get a track on the man and his family's habits. He'd initially thought Winston's request a little strange considering he normally only asked for information about people's computer habits. To ease his mind, Winston offered the man a large lump sum of money and no one, not even a straight-line private eye, could resist that much cold hard cash, so any additional questions were kept to himself.

They'd set up a meeting in a restaurant not too far from Winston's job so he slid on his jacket with the intention of taking an early lunch on his last day at work before heading out on his trip.

"Leaving so soon?" Jasmine stood in the doorway, her hands on her hips.

Damn. He'd hope to make it out before she made her rounds. "Yeah. I got a lunch date. I'll be back in an hour or so."

"Date?" She gave him a not so happy look.

"Not that kind of date. I'm meeting with a friend about some non-work related business." He picked up his keys, not making a move for the door in case she decided she had something else to say to him.

Her face turned to a scowl, not convinced that he wasn't going to see another woman.

"Get those thoughts out of your head." Her face clearly showed the thoughts racing through her mind. More than sure she was thinking he was going to see another woman, Winston tried to reassure her before her imagination ran too wild. "This is about my brother."

An eyebrow rose at his confession. "So you're going through with this?" Jasmine didn't know whether to be proud or scared. A lot could happen while he was gone, including things ending on a sour note.

"Yes I'm going through with this. I don't know what's going to happen but I'm ready to put this behind me." Winston hoped he sounded convincing. If she knew what he was planning once he got to Atlanta, she'd be way beyond pissed. "Look, I gotta run. We'll talk when I get home tonight."

"Yeah. Whatever." Jasmine turned, making sure he caught a good glimpse of her outfit before stepping back out into the hallway.

Winston's eyes followed the line of her long legs as she rounded the corner. He smiled knowing she was going to make him pay for canceling their lunch date. Right now though, footing that bill was the least of his concerns.

#

Winston ignored the soft hum of voices in the restaurant focusing his attention on the words on the menu. He folded the plastic covered pictures and words as the thin brown skinned man with dark brown hair and scars from years of bad acne approached his table.

"You're late," Winston said in a not so pleasant tone. He needed to get back to work and he was hoping to make this quick so that he could grab some lunch on the way back to the office. He so hated the food in this place.

"Nice to see you again too."

"You have what I need?" Not impressed, Winston took a sip from his coffee as the man pulled out the chair opposite his and took a seat.

"Right here." He pulled an envelope from the inside of his coat and placed it on the table.

Winston did the same. The two men exchanged envelopes. Collecting what he'd come here for, the man politely excused himself, leaving Winston at the table to review what his hard earned money could provide.

His hand traced the flap of the brown envelope, hovering over the metal prongs. This was it, the moment of truth. If he opened this envelope, then he'd have everything he needed to enact his plan. He took a moment to consider the repercussions of what he was plotting. Revenge could be so sweet and yet, he'd seen revenge go wrong for so many people he wondered if this was really worth it.

The longer he held the envelope, the more he flipped it around in his hand, the more he stared at it the more he knew he had to do this. This would be his big payback and no one would ever know.

Pulling up two metal flaps he opened the envelope and slid the stack of papers out. He flipped through the pages, reading the information. His friend had done a pretty good job of getting him what he'd asked for. As expected, Sheridan moved like clockwork. Leave by seven thirty in the morning and home by seven at night.

Sheridan had always said his wife would never work so the fact that Amira was a housewife came as no surprise. His friend had check DMV records and discovered that Amira had a state issued ID but no license, which meant she relied on others to get her where she needed to go. And she always wore loads of jewelry. From bangles to rings and earrings, she always donned ice.

The neighbors appeared to be good friends with Amira. They'd been by the house a couple of times during the week taking Amira and the two youngest children to the grocery store. They'd stayed for hours each day, working in the guesthouse on the backside of the property or out in the gardens. The three women sat in the back yard on Wednesday having tea.

He scanned the logs, looking for patterns of behaviors for the women as well as his brother. He mapped out his plan, circling key days and times to schedule his appearances. This might be easier than he'd previously thought.

His contact had also gathered information about Amira's friends. They were a colorful bunch at best. First was Carmen, the workaholic. Probably uses her job to get away from her whining controlling husband. Apparently she spent every ounce of free time away from work at the Malcolm residence.

Then there was Madison, the trophy wife. Husband

travels quite often, a number of suspected affairs; one child who is a total mess and possible heavily uses pills and alcohol. This was turning out to be good. He could use this information against them if either of them tried to confront him or tell his brother. He'd need them for his plan to work; he just hoped they were gullible enough to fall for it.

Flipping to the last page, Winston studied the words in red letters. His brother had a trip planned. He'd be out of town for a week, plenty of time for Winston to fly in, do what he planned to do and jet out before anyone suspected something was up. And with his brother out of the picture, he didn't have to worry about running into him.

Dialing the airline on his cell phone, Winston verified the flight information just to make sure the arrangements provided on the itinerary were correct. Then he made his own arrangements. The only loose end to handle would be Jasmine and that would be easy. She'd be glad to hear that he was going to pay his brother a visit. She didn't need to know the details of the trip so he'd definitely keep those to himself.

Sheridan and Amira

Tara sat on the couch in the Malcolm residence helping Nasir with his math problems. Baby girl sat at her feet playing with one of her dolls while the youngest Malcolm child rolled around in his playpen. She glanced up as Sheridan dragged his suitcase from the bedroom headed in the direction of the front door. She heard Amira in the kitchen putting the finishing touches on their lunch.

This was going to be an awkward meal, the last her sister and brother-in-law would have for a little over a week. Amira had invited Tara and Sheridan had invited Terrence so they all could sit together for this meal to help comfort Amira. She'd withdrawn as the day for Sheridan to leave on his business trip drew closer. They'd hoped having everyone here would ease her mind a little.

Sheridan closed the front door and entered the living room just as Amira stuck her head out of the kitchen signaling them that the food was ready. He yelled out to Terrence who'd retreated to the study to take a phone call. He then picked up his little one from the playpen and hugged him. He'd miss his little man while he was gone, but he was leaving his family in good hands. He just hoped Amira would be all right.

With his baby girl close on his heels and Tara and Nasir right behind them, Sheridan entered the kitchen. He placed his son in the high chair and slid into the chair at the head of the table. Waiting for everyone to take their places the members of the extended family held hands as Amira blessed the food.

Only the sounds of forks scraping across plates and lip smacking could be heard at the table. The smell of fried chicken, green beans, and hand whipped potatoes filled the room, the rich aromas adding to the flavor of each bite. Sheridan watched as Amira pushed her food around on her plate. He understood her loss of appetite but she couldn't continue like this.

He reached over, placing a hand on hers. She looked up at him, giving him a weak smile. His eyes didn't waver from his wife's as he excused them from the table. Sheridan led Amira into the bedroom, closing the door behind them. He stared at her, wanting to ease her pain but not quite knowing how.

"I don't know if I can do this," she finally said as a lone tear blazed a path down her cheek.

"Yes you can. You won't be alone. If you need anything just call Terrence or your sister." He brushed away a stray lock of hair as he cradled her face in his palms. "I'll call every night to make sure everything is okay."

"I know but…"

"Shh. There's no but. You can do this. We can do this.

I'll be back before you know it." Sheridan pulled his wife into a loving embrace. She was warm, her breath against his arm sending a wave of desire through his body.

No longer able to deny the urge to take her, Sheridan raised her chin. Losing himself in the endless pools of her eyes he closed the minute distance between them until their lips touched. He felt his desire for her ignite, causing his hands to slide the straps of her dress down her shoulders revealing bare flesh and full perky breast.

Knowing that he still had a couple of hours before he had to leave for the airport, he'd give his wife a little physical attention. He inched them closer to the center of the bed sliding her dress down her hips so that she could step out of it. As usual, she wasn't wearing any underwear.

Amira undressed him just as swiftly, wanting to feel the warmth of his body lying on top of hers. She tossed his shirt to the side of the bed, raking her nails over the defined muscles in his back. He released a low moan that sent a sensual shudder through her body. She worked quickly to unbutton his pants and with one foot she inched them down his legs. Sheridan kicked his way out of the khaki pants.

He rolled them over so that his ebony beauty straddled him. He pulled her closer, diving into the mounds of flesh with the two rich dark caps. He took his time licking, sucking, and kneading until his wife whimpered as he blew on the sensitive peaks. His tongue traced the flesh, his hands walking light paths down Amira's back.

He felt the pulsing between her legs quicken, the desire to have him joined with her rising with each touch of his body with hers. He smiled, gazing into her eyes as he shifted just enough so that his body danced at the entrance with hers. She closed her eyes, a slow lustful breath escaping as he danced around the place where in only a moment he'd become one with her. Her nails dug into his shoulders as he slowly entered her body.

They fit perfectly together, her body molding with his like the complementing sides of the yin and yang symbol. Amira rocked her hips, the sensation of bonding with her husband calming any apprehension she may have harbored. He continued to caress her body, his hands roaming freely across her curves as he searched for those special places that sent her riding waves of ecstasy each time they made love.

She felt one of his hands coming to rest on her stomach as the fingers of his other hand walked up her spine. His fingers played in her private jungle, his thumb coming to rest on the little pink pebble that would send her toppling over the edge of desire. She gasped as he drew circles on the sensual spot, her pace increasing with each gentle caress.

Sheridan held on to his wife as he lifted them from the bed. He knew exactly how she wanted this to end. She didn't need to tell him. He'd give her what her body desired in a way he knew she'd love. He broke their bond only long enough to position her on her knees at the edge of the bed. He stood behind her sliding her body back to his while trailing kissing over her shoulders.

He wrapped his fingers around her hips pulling her back to him while he pushed into her. She yelped as he hit her favorite spot. Her body shook as he held her there, captive, a slave to the pleasure and pain of bumping that special place. He drew back still keeping a firm grip on her hips, not allowing her to move without his permission. She squeezed as the tip of his body came to the entry of hers causing Sheridan to shake. But he held on, her teasing only making this all the more enjoyable for him.

He slipped back into the warm wet welcoming place, inching in a little at a time before drawing back again. When Amira picked up on the pattern he allowed her to take control. He reached around her, his attention again focusing on the pebble of pleasure hidden in the swollen folds of flesh. She quickened the pace, the sound of flesh pounding against flesh echoing through the room. Amira leaned forward her hands gripping the sheets, balling into fists. She buried her face in the goose down comforter as she reached that place where only Sheridan had ever been able to take her. She felt the desire mounting, the rich sound of his voice asking if she felt it too, covering her, adding fuel to the already flaming inferno fighting to crescendo until they both spontaneously combusted.

She squeezed once more as Sheridan gripped her by the shoulders and pulled her back. As he bumped that place inside, it sent her in a nosedive of desire, his name muffled by her face buried in the comforter as she pulled him along with her into that wonderful world of true orgasmic release. They both trembled, neither able to control the aftermath of what they'd just accomplished together.

Sheridan wrapped his arms around his wife's waist his weight resting against hers. She stretched out of the bed allowing him to lie on her back. She knew any minute now his legs would give way, but she wasn't ready to break the physical bond between them. Having him still inside of her was comforting, something she'd hold on to while he was away.

***

Sheridan grabbed the ringing phone from the cradle, hoping to get it before it woke Amira. He didn't know how they'd ended up spooning in the middle of the bed but at the moment it didn't matter.

"Hello?" Sheridan rolled over trying his best to keep his voice down so as not to wake his sleeping beauty. He looked over at the clock, realizing what Terrence was telling him. "Thanks for waking me. I'll be out in a few."

Sheridan hung up the phone, rolling over again. He draped his arm over Amira, nuzzling her neck. She was still sound asleep. Careful not to disturb her, Sheridan wiggled his way out of the bed and slipped into the bathroom to take a quick shower. He still smelled like her, like the love they'd made an hour or so ago. Though he'd miss having the scent of her clinging to his skin, he needed to get going if he was going to make his flight.

Standing in the shower, the warm water pelting his muscles, Sheridan thought about the next week without his family. He was just as worried about how he was going to make it as he was sure Amira was. They'd get through this somehow; it's not like they had much of a choice at this point. Still he was feeling just as apprehensive about this as Amira.

More than relaxed and smelling clean, Sheridan dried off and dressed. He knelt by the side of the bed watching as his dark chocolate angel slept. She'd wrapped her arms around his pillow probably because the scent of him still lingered in the cloth. Placing a kiss on her forehead, he pulled an envelope out of his jacket pocket and placed it on the nightstand next to the phone. He hoped the little card would bring her some comfort while he was away.

Quietly, Sheridan crept out of the bedroom, closing the door behind him. He didn't want to see her cry and he knew if he let her see him leave, she'd do just that. Better that he let her sleep.

"She all right?" Terrance asked as Sheridan entered the living room. He'd laid back in one of the royal blue chairs on the side of the coffee table, giving him the best view of the television.

"Yeah. She's asleep. Make sure you and Tara take care of her and the kids." Sheridan slid on the jacket to his suit and stood in the mirror tying his tie.

"I'm not going to let anything happen to them while you're gone. And I'm sure between Tara and her friends Amira will be just fine."

Tie straight, jacket buttoned, keys in hand, Sheridan took one last look around his living room. He heard the kids in the other room playing and his youngest son sat in his godfather's lap chewing on a teething ring.

"Well I guess I'm out."

"We got this Sheridan. Go handle your business."

Sheridan made his way over to where Terrence sat. He grabbed his son from the man, hugging him tight one last time. He relinquished the little boy to Terrence before dropping his head and walking out the front door.

ANA'GIA WRIGHT

Winston

Two gates down from where his brother's flight was scheduled to board, Winston slid down in his seat making sure the pages of the newspaper covered his face. The last thing he needed was for Sheridan to see him. He'd scheduled his flight to arrive a couple of hours before his brother's took off, giving him ample time to find his brother's gate and make sure he boarded that plane.

Over the top of the newspaper, Winston stared at the man standing at the counter. Sheridan appeared healthy, a little more physically fit since the last time he'd seen him, though Sheridan always stayed in fairly good shape. With a fresh haircut and a clean cut face, Winston knew he'd have to do some extra grooming if he was going to pull this off.

Sheridan turned in his direction but he covered his face with the paper. Waiting a few seconds more, he again looked over the top glad that his brother had turned his attention back to the numbers scrolling across the board behind the attendants. Winston watched as his brother stood in line waiting to board the plane with the other passengers. He chatted with a Caucasian man standing in line next to him. The two men handed the gate attendant their boarding passes and headed through the door to the plane.

Winston folded his newspaper as the last of the passengers entered the doorway and the gate attendant closed and locked the door. He made his way over to the window, waiting for the plane to pull away to taxi. When it backed up and rolled toward the line of planes waiting on the runway, Winston slung his bag over his shoulder to make his way to pick up his rental car. *So it begins.* He pulled out his cell phone, dialing the number to S&A Construction. When a young female voice picked up, Winston started the next stage of his plan.

"Good Afternoon. I was calling to set up an appointment with Mr. Sheridan Malcolm." The woman told him to hold on while she got his calendar. In the meantime, Winston moved two places closer to a beautiful dark haired woman with high cheekbones and a welcoming smile at the rental counter. Still four customers back, he again focused on the woman who'd returned to the phone.

"Actually, I'll only be in town for the week or so. I was hoping to speak with him while I was in town. Does he have anything available near the end of the week?" Instead of disappointment, he smiled as the woman informed him that Mr. Malcolm would be unavailable for at least ten days. She'd just given him the timetable he needed to make sure he did what he came to do and left before his brother suspected a thing.

Convincing the woman that he'd have to get back with her when he was available, he ended the phone call and stepped up to the counter.

"Can I help you sir?" The woman batted her eyes at him, flashing a slightly crooked smile.

"You can get me my rental car, and add your phone number to the bill." Winston pulled out a copy of his rental confirmation and his license and handed the information to the woman flirting with him.

Winston had made sure that his rental was the exact make and model of Sheridan's vehicle. It had taken him some time to find a place carrying a black Tahoe with the exact wheels that Sheridan had but with a little extra persuasion and a couple of hundred tacked on to his bill, he was able to find a company willing to fulfill his request.

Staring at the woman in the tight knee length navy blue skirt, Winston found her attractive in the round the way girl sort of way. Her dark brown hair framed her heart shaped face and he detected a dimple on the left side when she smiled. He liked the fact that she'd put on enough makeup to accentuate her features without appearing to have plastered on her face. She'd left the top three buttons of her shirt undone revealing a set of full round breasts. She made sure to lean over a little further to give him a good look at her assets.

"Let me get you to sign and initial right here."

Leaning over a little further still, she pointed to three places on the contract. She smiled at him taking in the way the number three preceded the W in his first name. The woman slid his key and a piece of paper with her phone number on it towards him, not relinquishing the items until his fingertips brushed with hers. Her cheeks flushed as a wave of desire raced through her body, and Winston was more that sure that the special place between her legs was growing moist.

"I'm free tomorrow night. Why don't you give me a call and we can hook up?" She gave him her best set of bedroom eyes making sure he understood what she offered.

Winston folded the piece of paper with the name and phone number in lavender on it and slid it into his pocket. Plucking the key from the counter he winked at the woman who took no shame in flirting with him.

"Make sure you keep your night free. I think I can manage to work something out to both of our satisfaction."

He blew a kiss at her before turning to exit the airport to board the shuttle to take him to his rental car. He'd almost forgotten how good it felt to flirt. Since hooking up with Jasmine, he hadn't really been in a situation to flirt. He'd stop going out alone and Jasmine wasn't exactly the type of woman who other women would try. She looked like she'd beat you down in a minute and truth be told, she probably would.

Climbing into the rented SUV, Winston looked over the directions to his brother's house. He thought about checking into his hotel first but decided that he wanted to get a look at the place that his brother called home. If he were lucky, maybe he'd even get a good look at Mrs. Malcolm.

He pulled out of the lot and headed down the access road towards the highway. He was really going to do this. He just hoped that Sheridan didn't make any unexpected visits.

Winston

Winston grabbed his bag and slung it over his shoulder as he shut the door to the rented truck. He walked toward the front door of the hotel more than pleased with himself. All of the pieces were falling into place. His brother was on a plane headed miles away. His woman was at home completely oblivious to every aspect of his plan.

Sheridan had had it all for far too long. Winston had always lived in his brother's shadow but now he'd get a taste of the life his brother stole from him. He stepped up to the counter, flashing his smile at the full figured woman behind the counter. Winston took all of her in, his tongue tracing over his lips as he scoped her out. This little trip to the Dirty Dirty was turning out to be a wakeup call for him. He'd almost forgotten about the healthy women of the south.

"Can I help you?"

He dropped the bag, leaning over the counter not trying to hide the fact that he was looking down her shirt. "Yeah, I have a reservation."

The woman's eyes roamed over him, scrutinizing his

every move. "And what might your name be?"

"Last name's Malcolm." He raised an eyebrow, waiting for her to ask the question sitting on the tip of her tongue.

The woman's cheeks turned bright red as he stared at her, obviously liking what he saw. "And what might Mr. Malcolm's first name be?"

"Sheridan." He watched as she typed in his information.

She glanced up occasionally as she waited for the computer to process his room key. She slid him the room print out asking for his signature on the paper.

Winston read over the information looking up at her, "I didn't reserve a suite."

"Is that a problem?" She slid him one of the office business cards with her name and phone number written on it in red ink.

He took the card, sliding it into the breast pocket of his suit before signing his name on the line. She'd given him a suite at the same rate as a regular room. He placed the pen down, pushing the paper back in her direction.

"What time do you get off?" He checked her hand, making sure she wasn't wearing a wedding ring. What Jasmine didn't know wouldn't hurt her. He might just have a little fun while he was here and maybe this one might also be able to help him out with his little plan.

"That all depends. What time you want to hook up?"

"How about eight-ish?"

She took the paper and dropped it in bin. Handing him the envelope containing his room key, she held on to it playing a little game of tug-of-war with the gorgeous man standing across the counter.

"Want me to come to your room?" Her fingers released the key, allowing Winston to slide it into his pocket.

"That won't be necessary. At least not for starters. My truck is the black one parked out front. Just meet me there." He turned, picking up the bag he'd dropped to the floor. Heading in the direction of the door, he felt her eyes boring into him from behind.

"Uh, Mr. Malcolm."

Winston stopped, looking back over his shoulder at the woman. She held a brown envelope out signaling him back to her.

"You did have a package." Holding the envelope out to him, she blew him a kiss as he slid it from her grasp.

"I'll see you in a few hours." He knew what was in the envelope. He'd had the investigator get some additional information about Amira's habits. This trip was for her, to make her doubt her husband, and to give Sheridan a taste of what he'd felt all of those years ago.

Settling in his room, Winston plopped down on the bed and slid the paperwork out of the envelope. He turned the television to ESPN before focusing his attention on the writing on the paper. He looked over the information, comparing it with the schedule he'd laid out. He made some minor changes based upon the new information, adjusting his rising time by an hour. If he made it to the house too early, he'd be spotted by whoever was taking the kids to school. Outside of that, everything else appeared to work out well.

Winston stretched, reaching over and setting the alarm clock for two p.m. That would give him a few hours of sleep before going to scope out Sheridan's home before the kids got out of school. By the paperwork, Amira's friends should be stopping through so maybe he'd get a good look at them.

He laid his head on the pillow, watching the weekend's scores scroll across the bottom of the television. His eyes grew heavy and before he knew it a welcomed sleep pulled him under.

Before he'd slipped too far into dreamland, the ringing cell phone on the nightstand jarred him from the light slumber. He patted for it, still not quite ready to open his eyes. When he located the contraption, he flipped it open, not taking time to look at the caller ID to see who it w

"What?"

Winston's eyes flew open at the sound of a female voice on the other end of the line replying *excuse me*. "My bad, I was half sleep."

He listened, as she questioned why he hadn't called when he first got in. "Look, I just got to the hotel. I got caught up at the airport and there was a line at the hotel. You know its check out time."

She didn't like his answers but had no reason to suspect that anything was going on. His excuses made sense and it was check out time. Still he heard her doubt.

"Look, can I call you back. I'm trying to get some sleep before I try to find my brother." He rolled his eyes as she questioned why he was rushing her off the phone. Winston smacked himself on the head, a reminder to next time check the caller id.

"Jasmine," he tried to interrupt but she wasn't hearing him, "Jasmine!" When she stopped, he continued, "I had a long, horrible flight. I'm tired. Can we finish this later?"

Reluctantly she agreed but she made him promise to call as soon as he woke up. With the promise laid out, he hung up the phone. Rolling over onto his side, he pressed the off button on the remote control and laid his head back to once again try to get some sleep.

ANA'GIA WRIGHT

Carmen and Madison

C armen pulled a lilac blouse from the sales rack, holding the fabric up the light to get a good look at it. She and Madison had headed out early to get a little shopping done before stopping by to help Amira with her orders. They both needed a break. They loved their friend dearly but since Sheridan had gone on his trip, they'd spent more hours with Amira than either of them cared to stomach again.

She grabbed two more of the same blouse, one in blue and the other in green, before looking up to locate a pair of pants to complete the outfit. Heading towards a rack near the front of the store, Carmen caught a glimpse of a familiar face. She scooted behind a pillar watching as a man looking a lot like Sheridan flirted with a woman in the food court.

Without taking her eyes off of the couple, she rambled through her purse for her cell phone. Flipping it open, she pressed the speed dial button for her partner in crime.

"Where are you?" Carmen's mouth dropped open as the man whispered something in the woman's ear. She snickered, placing her hand over her ample bosom, a clear attempt to draw his attention there.

Shaking her head, Carman again came to her senses. She responded to the woman yelling into her ear. "Put your clothes on and get out here! Now!"

Her mouth opening even wider, Carmen cut off Madison's rambling. "I can't explain it. You need to see this for yourself."

She put down the items she'd planned to purchase, walking closer to the door to keep the moving couple within her sight. With her eyes locked on them, Carmen watched as the man turned the woman around. He held her gaze for a moment before leaning down and planting a wet one-smack dab on her lips.

Carmen turned around at the gasp from behind. She pulled Madison out of the doorway, hoping the couple hadn't seen them.

"Oh hell naw. I'm going to give him a piece of my mind."

"Whoa. Calm down Madison. We don't know for sure that's Sheridan." Carmen continued to stare at the two people in the food court on the other side of the mall.

"What do you mean that's not Sheridan? Look at him, laid all up on that girl. I'm going over there?"

"No you're not. Let's just watch and see what happens."

Holding hands, the couple grabbed their bags and headed toward the mall entrance.

"I'm not going to just let him get away with this." Madison's eyes widened when the guy intertwined his fingers with the chick in the black mini skirt and low cut halter-top. It was barely seventy degrees outside and she was more than sure that hoochie had to be cold.

"Neither am I," Carmen replied. "Let's go."

Carmen dashed out of the store with Madison only a few paces behind her. They stayed out of site, hiding behind pillars, pretending to shop at the kiosk in the isles whenever the couple stopped to look into a window. They still hadn't gotten a good enough look at the man to be positive it was Sheridan but Madison was more than convinced her eyes weren't deceiving her.

They followed the man and woman to the doors of the mall, hovering in a crowd of people waiting by the door. They watched as the man helped the woman into a black Tahoe before he climbed into the driver's seat and backed out of the parking space. Coming towards them, the two women ducked behind a bush. Unfortunately in their attempt to keep from being seen, they didn't get a good look at the license plate.

"I never thought he'd do this to Amira." Madison, her hand on her hip, narrowed her eyes as the SUV headed up the ramp and through the green streetlight.

"We can't say anything about this." Adamant on keeping this to themselves until they had confirmation, Carmen just shook her head.

"What do you mean we can't say anything? That woman's at home, believing that her husband is out of town on a business trip and he's still here running around with some hussy."

"Madison, can you really be sure that was Sheridan. I don't want to start anything, especially since Amira is at home alone."

Madison didn't care what Carmen said. That was Sheridan. And if he thought he was going to get away with this, he was dead wrong. "Come on. We need to figure out how to break this to Amira."

Carmen didn't follow Madison immediately. She still wanted to be cautious about accusing Sheridan of cheating. Something inside told her that there was more going on than what they'd just seen. And she still wasn't one hundred percent positive that was Sheridan they'd just seen. Looking up at the light once again, knowing that the couple they'd just seen was long gone, Carmen went back inside of the mall.

A pair of angry eyes met her as Madison glared at her. Carmen took in her obvious pleasure at knowing that Sheridan was cheating. For once, Carmen wondered if there might be some other reason for Madison wanting to tell Amira even though she was sure she still held some doubts if the man they'd just seen really was Sheridan.

Carmen followed Madison into the food court taking a seat at a table in the corner. She leaned back, watching a couple of teenagers obviously skipping school.

"I still can't believe what we just saw." Madison sat across from Carmen, opening a bottle of Perrier water and talking a gulp.

"And what exactly, and I do mean exactly, did we just see?"

"What's with you? You were standing there just I was. You saw the way he was all up on that little sassy thang." She eyed her friend not believing she was trying to act like she hadn't seen anything.

"Look Madison, before you go getting all happy and thinking you have a chance with Sheridan," which Carmen knew hell would freeze over before that happened, "we need to find out if there's some logical explanation."

"What kind of logical explanation can there be for that!"?

"Lower you voice woman, we don't need the whole world up in our business." Carmen smiled at the group of women who'd turned in their direction. When they went back to their conversation, she leaned in, keeping her voice down. "How do we know that was Sheridan?"

"And what makes you so sure that wasn't Sheridan?"

"Come on Madison. Why would Sheridan cheat on Amira? She cooks, cleans, and takes care of the kids. Twenty-four hours a day she's at his beck and call. Have you ever even seen them fight?" None of this made sense. There had to be some sort of explanation. She just wished she knew what it was.

"That has nothing to do with it." Madison pursed her lips at Carmen. She was taking all of the joy out of crushing little Miss Perfect's dream.

"It has everything to do with it. How many kids do they have? Apparently he's getting everything he needs at home. And with the way you throw yourself at him every time Amira turns her back, if he wanted to cheat, then he'd have had ample opportunity to do it before now."

"Then you explain what we just saw." She glared at the woman sitting across from her, waiting on this magical explanation that would make everything better.

"How do we know that wasn't an old family friend?"

"Ex-girlfriend maybe," Madison replied under her breath. She cocked her head to the side before responding, "Get real Carmen. Ain't nobody kissin' a family friend like that."

"Well, maybe not but maybe that guy just looked a lot like Sheridan. Come on, everybody has somebody out here that looks just like them. It happens all of the time." Another possibility. Unfortunately, Carmen wasn't buying that one herself so she was more than sure Madison was going to have a comeback for it.

"If you say so."

"Look, there's one way to resolve this." Carmen pulled out her phone and dialed Sheridan's assistant. She waited for the woman to answer the phone. "Hi Kisha, this is Carmen, Amira's friend. I need to ask you a question."

She listened as the woman put her on hold. When she returned Carmen asked, "Did Sheridan go on his business trip?"

"So?" Madison didn't care what the woman had said. That was Sheridan and no one was going to make her believe otherwise.

"So, Sheridan got on that plane. He checked in a few hours ago?" Carmen nodded at Madison as the woman on the other end of the line confirmed that Sheridan had gone on his trip.

"That doesn't mean anything. If he called from a cell phone, he could be anywhere."

Thanking Sheridan's assistant and hanging up the

phone Carmen replied, "Leave it alone Madison. Until we can be positive, I don't want you saying anything to Amira about this."

"How are we ever gonna be sure that was'n him?"

"If it's so important, we can try to figure out a way to find out if Amira saw Sheridan board the plane."

"You know they don't 'low nobody without a ticket to go to 'dem gates. Ain't no way to make sure he got on that plane." The increase in depth of Madison's southern drawl indicated her irritation with Carmen trying to convince her not to tell Amira about this.

"Maybe she talked to him. I'm sure when he got to the hotel he called her. Come on. Let's see what we can find out. But I'm warning you, keep this to yourself." Carmen's expression clearly indicated she wasn't playing with Madison. If she so much as breathed a word of this to Amira before they were sure, she'd pay.

"You know, there's very little you could do to keep me from tellin'." Madison fanned her hand, pretending to feel flush from the underlying implication.

"Oh really," she didn't want to have to do this but if Madison wanted to play hardball, then she was all for it. "And how do you think your husband would feel knowing that his wife was a pill popping, alcoholic, adulterer?"

"You wouldn't."

"Try me." Carmen got up from the table and walked away, leaving a clearly stunned Madison sitting at the table with her mouth hung down to her knees.

Madison knew Carmen was serious. When it came to

Amira, she'd do anything to make sure her friend stayed happy even if it meant ruining someone else's life. Not that she blamed Carmen. But Madison was going to make sure that if Sheridan did become available, she'd be at the top of his list of new suitors. Madison got up and followed Carmen in the direction of her car.

Amira, Carmen & Madison

C armen followed Madison up the front stairs to the Malcolm residence. She'd been quiet on the ride over, really not wanting to go along with this but not having much of a choice. If Sheridan was cheating on Amira, things were probably going to get ugly. And there was no telling what Madison might say to get their friend thinking that her husband wasn't being exactly faithful.

As Madison reached for the doorbell, Carmen stopped her. She looked the woman straight in the eyes, wanting her to understand the seriousness of the words she was going to say. Madison glared back at her but Carmen refused to back down.

Crossing her arms over her chest she began, "I'm warning you Madison, if you so much as hint at what we saw today, I'll have your ass."

"I must say, you are being quite protective, aren't you? Seems to me you may have more to lose than lil Amira."

"What are you talking about?"

"Come on now. I know why you spend so much time

over here making sure little Miss Innocent's home stays whole."

"What are you trying to say?" Carmen didn't like it when Madison tried to manipulate her. Amira had warned her to be careful what she said and did around Madison. After they'd had that talk, she'd started paying attention to Madison's snide remarks and hidden accusations.

"You need somebody to look up to. Amira's perfect little world gives you hope that one day you and that husband of yours could actually have something."

"You know what, I'm not getting into this with you. You're just jealous that other people have good marriages unlike that sham of a I don't even know what to call it that you've got going on." A little perturbed, Carmen rang the doorbell. She knew Madison was just pushing her buttons but this was neither the time nor the place. They had business to tend to and this conversation could definitely wait.

Plastering warm smiles on their faces as the locks turned, Carmen and Madison's eyes lit up when Amira swung the front door open.

"Well look at this," Amira said adjusting her youngest child to the other hip.

"We just thought you might want some company." Carmen opened her arms and Amira relinquished her baby boy to his Godmother.

Madison walked past them both headed toward the sitting room attached to the living room. Carmen and Amira just shook their heads, choosing not to acknowledge the childish behavior of the third member of their unusual trio. She still had her panties in a bunch because Amira and Sheridan had asked Carmen to be their youngest child's Godmother instead of her.

"Just leave it alone girl, just leave it alone." Carmen followed Amira into the sitting room. She plopped down in the rocking chair by the window while Amira sat next to a pouting Madison.

"When are you going to get over this?" Amira asked Madison, concerned that after all of this time, she was still upset about the Godmother thing.

"Why, I don't rightly know what you're referring to."

"You know damn well what I'm talking about. Are you going to stay mad forever? We thought you'd be relieved considering how much of a handful baby girl is." Amira hadn't wanted Madison to be her daughter's Godmother but when her sister and Carmen had declined the position, Madison came to be the last resort. Though, legally she'd only end up with the little girl if something happened not only to Amira and Sheridan but also Terrance, the notion still bothered Amira some nights.

They waited for the woman to reply but when it became obvious that she'd keep her feeling to herself, Amira decided to change the subject. "So what do I owe this visit from my two best friends?"

"We just stopped by to see how you were holding up and to make sure you have everything you need," Carmen replied, rocking the little boy lying across her lap. His eyes were slowly but surely closing and she was convinced he'd be asleep before they finished the conversation.

"Well I'm making it. I guess. Kinda quiet around here

though."

"What do you mean quiet? With that one," Madison pointed at the little boy, "how can you say any place is quiet?"

"Not quiet like that. I mean," Amira's eyes darted to the door, "I keep waiting for Sheridan to sneak in like he does around this time."

"Sneak in?"

"Yeah," Amira tried to hide her devilish grin but Madison caught a glimpse of the embarrassment her friend exhibited.

"Spill it, young lady."

"Let's just say that one right there," Amira cut her eyes at her now sleeping baby, "was a result of one of Sheridan's lunch breaks."

"Okay. That was too much information." Carmen snickered at her friend, understanding completely.

"You two are too much." Madison chose not to ask any further questions. The last thing she wanted to hear about was Amira and Sheridan's midday rolls in the hay.

Amira stood and made her way over to the window, turning her attention to the blue skies. It was such a nice day and yet internally her heart was covered with cloudy skies. She wrapped her arms around her midsection, fighting back tears.

"You okay hun?" Madison asked the question but kept her distance. She assumed her friend was thinking about the next few days without her husband.

"Yeah. I miss him so much already." She lowered her head, thinking about how this would be the first time in a long time she'd be sleeping alone in their bed.

"How long is he planning to be gone?"

Carmen eyed Madison, giving her a clear warning. Madison's eyes darted from Carmen's to Amira's and back to the frown on Carmen's face.

"At least until next week. Maybe longer." Her voice held the sorrow of being without the man who'd always been there to protect her.

"Don't worry your pretty little head. How about we get you out of the house tomorrow? We can take the little one to the park or maybe even the zoo."

"I don't know. I still have plenty to do around here?"

"We won't take no for an answer," Carmen interjected, "we're not going to let you just sit around here all day moping. Whatever you have to do can wait a few hours."

Amira faced her friends. Taking in the serious but caring looks, she let out a huff before reluctantly agreeing.

"Then it's settled." Carmen scooped the sleeping child from her lap and placed him in the playpen. She made her way over to where her friend stood. Amira was nearly in tears so she offered a comforting hug.

"It's going to be all right. If you need anything, you know where to find us."

Though Carmen couldn't see it, Amira smiled at the reassurance her friend offered. Madison joined them and together they formed a little circle. Friends for life is what they were and although they had their differences, they'd always be there when someone needed them.

Winston

Winston peered out of the window of his rental truck, watching the three women in the front window of Sheridan's home. From where he sat and with the aid of the binoculars, he observed the sadness in the eyes of the woman standing in plain view in front of the glass. She looked to be on the verge of tears, but not distraught enough to have been told that her husband was cheating.

He waited for her to show some additional reaction, hoping that maybe the words were just sinking in. Instead, she turned to face her friends and walked into their welcoming hug.

"Damn, they must not have told her."

He continued to take in the sight of the dark chocolate diva as she stood in the doorway of the house seeing her friends off. His tongue traced his lips as he imagined running his hands over her hourglass figure. The v-neck sweater she wore hugged her voluptuous breast and by the look of her nipples protruding through the knit material, she wasn't wearing a bra. Her pants accentuated her narrow waist and he found his attention drawn down to the fullness of her thighs. The only out of place aspect of her outfit were the fuzzy red slippers on her feet.

Watching this woman standing on the porch giving her final goodbyes to her friends, Winston could see how Sheridan had fallen for her. She was way beyond attractive and stacked in just the right places just like they used to like them. She knew how to dress, always a plus when you wanted to go out and show your woman off.

He wasn't quite sure about her friends though. Pretty sure they hadn't realized he'd been following them through the mall, he'd listened in on some of their conversations about Amira and Sheridan. Winston was more than convinced that the thin woman with the blonde hair wearing so much jewelry he'd have sworn she was a Tiffany's model had her eye on Sheridan. He even considered using her, making a move just to see if something might happen. He filed that thought away for safekeeping. If by the time he was headed home his plan had fallen apart, he knew where she lived. A quick pit stop on the way to the airport and his brother's life would crumble like a week old cookie.

Winston slid down in the seat as the two women pulled out of the driveway and rounded the corner. He'd backed into the driveway of one of the neighboring houses so that from the doorway of the Malcolm residence he couldn't be seen because of the bushes.

Winston observed Amira still standing on the porch watching her friends drive away. She turned in his direction, as if she felt someone watching her. Her gaze remained locked in his direction, sending a cold shudder racing down his spine. He ducked down, thinking maybe somehow she had seen him. But she turned and walked back into the house, closing the door behind her.

She entered the front room again, lifting the sleeping child from the playpen. She walked over to the window, staring again in his direction before sliding down the blinds and pulling the curtains closed.

Sure that she was no longer watching him, he started the vehicle and pulled out into the street. He crept past the Belflore's home, taking note that the car the two women had driven away in was parked in front of the garage at the top of the hill. He exited the subdivision, hopping on the main street and heading in the direction of his hotel. He'd have to step up his plan a notch and he knew just how to do that.

Winston

Circling the movie theatre parking lot, Winston followed behind Madison's sleek silver Mercedes SL65 AMG. He kept his distance, making sure she didn't suspect that he was following her. When she pulled into a parking spot he turned down the next isle over, pulling into a space near the end of the row.

He waited for the two women to exit the vehicle and walk toward the box office before he climbed from the truck. Shutting the door, he opted to not arm the alarm just in case the chirping caught their attention. Staying out of sight until the two women paid for their tickets and entered the building; Winston made his way to the ticket booth.

"Hey man, the two chicks that just bought tickets. What movie they seein'?"

The young man, probably no older than sixteen told Winston the name of the movie and proceeded to give him a ticket to the same show. Slipping through the door, and keeping his distance, Winston watched as Amira's friends grabbed some popcorn and their drinks and headed into their theatre. Now all he needed to do was find him a cute little honey and he'd definitely give them a show.

Leaning against a pillar, no longer feeling the need to hide from prying eyes, Winston caught the attention of a tall brown skinned woman in a skintight pair of black leather pants, five-inch stiletto heels and a leather vest top. She'd just hung her jacket over her shoulders to ward off a chill.

The two locked eyes and before he could react to the stunning baby blues staring back at him, she blew a kiss in his direction. He winked, flashing a smile at her before cutting through the crowd to holla.

Winston watched the young woman fight back a smile as the distance between them diminished. He stepped up to her, giving her outfit the once over before leaning in and asking, "How you doing?"

She giggled, covering her chest with her hand, drawing his eyes down in that direction. He glanced back up at her, inhaling the aroma of her floral perfume.

"Well, are you going to tell me your name?" Winston finally asked when he realized she wasn't going to answer his question.

"Tawanna."

"Tawanna huh?" He eyed her again trying to decide if that really was her name. Not that it mattered. She'd do nicely. "Care to join me?" With one suave move, he offered her his arm.

"I'd love to." She slid her arm through his, allowing him to lead the way into the theatre.

As they entered the now dimming theatre to find seats, Winston scanned the crowed searching for the two women playing an intricate part in his plan. Allowing his new friend to lead the way, he spotted the two women huddled up near the top of the theatre. His eyes turned away just as the blonde haired woman pointed in his direction.

Winston reached out, touching his new friend on the elbow. He pointed at two seats a few rows down from where Amira's friends sat. They slid into the row claiming the last two seats near the wall. He fought the urge to turn and look up. He felt the women's eyes boring into his back, a clear indication that the pieces of his plan were falling into place.

He made small talk with the woman, trying way too hard to keep his attention. He reached into his jacket pocket, pulling out his cell phone and looking down at the number on the caller id. He knew sooner or later Jasmine was going to call.

Leaning over, brushing a number of curls out of the way, Winston whispered, "Want some popcorn?"

"Sure," was her only reply as she turned to face him brushing her lips across his.

Winston pecked her on the cheek, making for a good show for his patsies. He made his way through the now forming crowd at the bottom of the staircase, exiting the theatre and getting into line to get the popcorn.

He pulled his cell phone out, dialing into his voice mail. He listened as Jasmine came this close to cursing him out. He'd been meaning to call her in the last couple of days but following around Amira's friends had become all consuming.

For them to for the most part be housewives, neither of the women stayed home. He'd been able to scope out a number of the blonde haired woman's extracurricular activities that mostly centered on her pool boy or the butler. Amira's other friend, the browned skinned woman, who didn't know how to wear anything except suits, spent most of her time on the phone walking back and forth in front of the bay window in her home. Apparently, the people in this neighborhood hadn't heard of being discrete or curtains.

Dialing Jasmine's cell number, he waited for her first words which he was more than sure would be where the hell have you been and why haven't you called.

He only snickered when those exact words flew from her mouth long before he got the opportunity to say one word. He allowed her to rant and rave and basically curse him out before he attempted to half explain what he'd been doing.

With all of the frustration out and Jasmine a tad bit calmer than shed been when she first answered the phone, Winston spoke. "I miss you baby."

He moved up in line allowing a little girl holding her younger brother's hand to go ahead of him while he tried to finish up his phone call with Jasmine.

"I know baby, but I've had a lot to do. I've been trying to work on some things concerning my brother." He waved at the little girl when she grabbed her popcorn and nearly dragged the little boy back over to where a lady dressed in jeans and a sweatshirt stood.

Still on the phone, he pointed to the combo containing a large popcorn and drink. He caught the bedroom eyes from the girl at the counter but chose to ignore the gesture.

"No baby, I haven't talked to him yet. He's been busy

and I just haven't caught up with him." He handed the girl the money for the food. "Look, I gotta go. I'll call you when I get back to the hotel." Damn she asked a lot of questions. He hoped she didn't ask where he was.

For the first time he could remember, Jasmine let him off of the phone without twenty additional questions. It caught him off guard, almost making him question if something was going on, though considering what he was up to, he had no right to question anyone else's motivation in a relationship.

Deciding to worry about all of that later, he picked up the popcorn and soda from the counter and made his way back into the theatre. He had enough to be concerned with right about now. Ole girl seemed to be more than willing to please him and maybe he could use that to his advantage. Climbing up the stairs again to the seat next to this brown cutie, he'd see how far she was willing to go to please him after the movie was over.

Carmen and Madison

Normally, Carmen was the more rational woman of the group but even she had her limits. She stared at the man she too was now convinced was Sheridan as he hugged up with some woman in the movie theatre. She felt so stupid. Madison was right all along. Sheridan was cheating on Amira. Well, she wasn't about to let him get away with it.

"What's going through your mind over there?" Madison had watched a number of emotions cross her friend's face in the last ten minutes. She'd tried to tell Carmen that that was Sheridan they'd seen in the mall a couple of days earlier but of course Carmen, being Carmen, wanted more proof. Well now she had it.

"I can't believe you were right."

"Believe it hun. As much as I didn't want it to be the truth, you cain't deny what's going on down there." Though she continued to look at Carmen, Madison pointed to the couple a few rows down whispering back and forth during the movie.

She sounded so smug but she was so right. "This still

doesn't make any sense. After all Amira does for him, why would he do this to her?"

"You know that could be the problem," Madison turned her gaze down towards the subject of their conversation, watching as he ran his hands through the curls of the young lady's hair. "Maybe Sheridan wants a woman who allows him to be the man."

"What are you talking about," Carmen raised her voice though she hadn't meant to. When she realized that she was disturbing the other people in the theatre, she leaned over closer to Madison, "Amira does everything a wife is supposed to do, including letting her husband bring home the bacon. And you saw the way she reacted about Sheridan's midday visits. If she isn't doing something right, then I'd like to know what it is."

Prepared to respond, Madison grabbed Carmen by the hand as the man they'd been watching turned the young lady to face him. They knew what was coming, and just as they suspected, he pulled her closer, planting a sloppy wet kiss on her lips.

"That's it," Carmen said through gritted teeth. She pulled off her rings and started on her earrings. "I'm going down there."

"Wait," this time Madison stopped the intrusion, "Let's see how far he takes this." She continued to stare at the couple as the man's hands roamed over the woman's shoulders then disappeared out of her sight. She could only imagine where they'd ended up.

Neither Madison nor Carmen watched the movie. Their attention remained focused on the man and the woman drooling all over each other. They'd fed each other popcorn, drinking from the same cup of soda, even through the same straw. The woman spent most of the movie with her head resting on the man's shoulders and by the end; she'd basically draped herself over him.

They didn't move as the credits started to roll and the couple stood. When they reached the end of the isle and began their decent, Madison stood and turned to her friend.

"Now let's see where they go."

The two women followed behind the man and the woman still acting too friendly to be just acquaintances. Madison slid behind the driver's seat of her vehicle as Carmen continued to hide behind the line of SUV's parked further down the row, keeping an eye on the people they were following. She dashed in the direction of Madison as the man helped the woman into the black Tahoe.

Jumping into the car they pulled out of the parking lot two vehicles behind the SUV.

"Can you believe he had the nerve to drive his own truck? The least he could have done was drive her car or borrow one." Carmen still wanted to believe that this was a mistake, but she'd gotten a close enough look at the man when he'd allowed the woman to walk ahead of him to know that it was definitely Sheridan.

"He's not expecting anyone to be following him. As far as he knows, we're at the house tending to Amira. Sheridan knows how she gets when he's away even for a couple of days." Madison changed lanes, keeping up with the lane changes of the SUV ahead of them.

"That's still no excuse for not being careful. It's almost like he's trying to get caught."

"Hadn't thought about that. Look." Madison pointed in the direction of a Marriot Residence Inn, "They're turning in."

"No way." Carmen's mouth dropped as the realization of what was about to happen sunk in.

"I hate to admit it but I think we have our answer for how far he plans to take this."

"Pull around but stay out of sight."

Madison chose not to comment on the order Carmen gave. Instead, she pulled to the side, waiting on the Tahoe to either pull into a parking space or continue around the corner. The man driving pulled to a stop in front of the last building, parking in the spot right in front of the door. From where they sat, Madison and Carmen had the perfect view of the door to the room.

Silently they both prayed that he'd just drop the young lady off and head on his way but when he escorted her to the door, his hand firmly on her behind, that wish fizzled into a lost hope. The couple stood at the door, hands tracing curves, sliding between legs while their lips remained locked.

The man slid a key from his jacket pocket, not breaking the lip lock with the woman. Her hands disappeared beneath the back of his jacket as he inserted the key into the lock. He lifted her, her legs wrapping around his waist as he opened the door, stepped inside and closed it behind them.

Carmen's hands balled into fist as the rage bubbled within. "We have to tell her," she said, taking in deep breaths and counting to ten to calm her nerves.

"I told you that before." Madison turned around in a

parking spot and pulled away. The last thing they were going to do was confront Sheridan. That didn't mean that they weren't going to spill this to Amira though.

"How are we going to tell her?" Carmen laid her head back on the headrest and closed her eyes. Amira was going to be more than heartbroken when they told her. And with all of those kids.

"I don't rightly know. But I do know that we need to tell her as soon as possible before Sheridan has a chance to cover his tracks." Madison crossed a busy intersection and took the access road heading in the direction of their neighborhood.

It was almost seven and the sun had set while they'd been in the movies. It was near the end of the week so plenty of partygoers lined the club entrances. Madison nearly ran into the back of a BMW that stopped to make a turn into a shopping center, her mind planning what she was going to say to Amira.

The funny thing was she expected to feel some sort of vindication now that she knew the truth. Sheridan had always been Mr. Perfect, pampering his wife every chance he got. He seemed too good to be true and if it was one thing Madison knew, if it appeared too good to be true then it probably was.

She finally had her chance at that hunk of dark chocolate but now, knowing that she had to be the one to break that woman's heart, she didn't want him anymore. He could satisfy her physical desires, but knowing what he'd done to her friend made every naughty thought about him seem that much more wrong.

Turning into the subdivision Madison didn't know how

they'd do this but by this time tomorrow, her friend would know the truth about Sheridan Malcolm.

What's good for one...

DOUBLETAKE

Winston

Between the sleeping pills and the alcohol she'd consumed, a bomb exploding couldn't have jarred Amira from her slumber. She lay curled up like a baby in the bed she shared with her husband, the sheets covering most of her body. The drugs and alcohol held her mind in such a captive state that she didn't notice the warm body sliding into the bed.

The man rolled her over onto her back, his hands tracing the line of her chin. He trailed kisses down her neck, pulling the sheets down to reveal her bare shoulders and breast. He continued his journey, savoring the woman's rich chocolate body. He took his time, taking pleasure in her body's response to his touch. Amira didn't make a sound but her nipples became pebbles as his tongue brushed against them.

He slid a hand beneath the sheets to find the bush between her legs exposed. Spreading her thighs, he slid a finger inside, finding her body warm, wet, and wanting. He continued to please her body though she continued to lie limp beneath him. He'd seen the bottle of pills on the nightstand when he'd crept into the bedroom. He'd even finished off the last swallow of the brown liquid in the glass next to the bottle. The combination of the two and she wouldn't remember a thing.

Assured that her body would accept his freely, no marks left for evidence, the man slid his body into hers. He hadn't expected the pulsing to start so soon, but something about this woman did something to him. He raised her hips, slowly drawing back until the tip of his body danced at the entrance of hers. He expected her to wake, to reach up and pull him back inside. He wanted her to enjoy in the ecstasy he experienced. But she didn't.

He reentered her body, keeping a slow steady pace, letting the excitement build until he was forced to increase the lover's tempo as his body burned with lust. He slipped and slid in and out of her body, dropping her hips back to the bed. He gripped the edge of the mattress, his fingers tightening as he pounded in and against the limp beauty beneath him. He was almost there and she was oblivious to what was going on. What a shame.

He continued, his muscles tightening, the warmth from her body driving him to the edge. It was coming, building, forcing him to quicken the pace to the point where he was sure the woman laying beneath him would open her eyes, rake her nails down his back, call his name. He hit the wall of bliss with his seed racing from his body into this beauty. He collapsed, quickly rolling over, not wanting to crush her with his weight.

Taking a moment to catch his breath he calmed down enough to turn and look at the woman with her arms and legs spread over the burgundy sheets. The moonlight bathed her dark skin. It caused an unusual glow that he couldn't quite comprehend. She looked like an angel lying there, helpless. His eyes grew wide as the truth slammed into his mind.

He ran from her, moving as quickly as possible to the other side of the room. He threw on his clothes, no longer able to look at her. He covered her body with the sheets, the least he could do after what he'd just done. Pulling his hands out of his pocket with the keys in a tight grip and slipping out of the bedroom, he closed the door behind him. He leaned back against it, his chest heaving up and down as panic set it.

The only thought racing through his mind, *I can't believe I just slept with my brother's wife.*

Needing to get as far away from this place as possible, Winston walked past the kitchen heading for the front door. He'd almost made it past the sofa when two tiny brown eyes caught his. He placed a finger over his lips indicating for the little boy not to make a sound. He had to act fast. If he were lucky, the little boy would mistake him for his father. He ushered the little girl in princess pajamas back into the open bedroom door on the other side of the hall. He tucked the little girl back into his bed, careful to not say a word. He didn't want to wake any of the other kids.

Winston slipped out of the room, waving good-bye to the brown eyes still locked on him. Closing the door, he rushed down the hallway and out of the front door. He was glad no one else had seen him. This was bad, real bad. What Sheridan had done was wrong but if he ever found out about this…

Winston drove around for hours, trying to clear his head. He'd come down here with the intention of making Sheridan's life a little less pleasant. He'd accomplished that, arousing suspicion through his wife's friends. But he hadn't meant to cross the line. Even though he suspected something had been going on between his brother and his ex that was teenaged stuff. He was toying not only with his brother's life but the lives of his wife and children. Bad, bad idea.

Pulling into the parking lot of the hotel he was staying in Winston had to get out of here. He was disgusted with himself for what he'd done. The only good thing out of this is that Amira was virtually unconscious. Hopefully, she wouldn't remember anything and he could just go on with his life. He couldn't entertain thoughts of trying to work things out with Sheridan right now. All he wanted to do was forget any of this had happened.

Winston packed his bag, throwing clothes into his suitcase and dragging it down the hall toward the main lobby. He paid his bill, still looking over his shoulder. He couldn't shake the feeling of eyes watching him; eyes of the little boy that looked just like his brother and him.

This was crazy. He pulled himself together long enough to get to the airport. Winston patted his jacket pockets, looking for a copy of his receipt for the rented truck. Since he was returning it early, he wanted to get the rest of the time credited to his account. Pulling the paper from his pocket and unfolding it, he realized that the business card the girl at the hotel had given him was missing. Shit!

He searched, hoping it was in one of the other pockets. No luck. Damn, he must have dropped it somewhere. Oh well, he'd check the pockets of his clothes when he got home. The last thing he needed to have happen was Jasmine finding the card with the phone number on it. He'd never hear the last of it.

Since he hadn't really decided when he was leaving, he didn't have a flight. For a little extra money, he managed to get the last first class seat on the next flight out. It wasn't leaving for a few hours so he had plenty of time to think about what he'd done.

Stupid stupid stupid. Why? Why after all of this time did he still feel the need to stay one up on his brother? For the first time, he saw what Jasmine was talking about. This competition, this jealousy between him and his brother had been festering within him for all of these years. It was his fault that he and Sheridan didn't have a relationship. It was his fault that he hadn't been able to truly commit to Jasmine. Until he dealt with this betrayal that he felt, this Sheridan owes me mentality, he'd continue to live his pathetic life.

Sitting in one of the many bars in the airport, Winston thought about his life. The little voice in his head kept repeating; *money can't buy happiness*. His boys use to tell him that all the time. Too bad it had taken this, him making the biggest mistake of his life for him to truly understand. Money was nothing without someone you could share it with. It was nothing without family. Money can't comfort you when you're sick. Money can't teach you how to love. It can blind you; make you wish you had friends. Make you believe that companionship isn't important. But when it all came down to it, he didn't need money: he needed his family.

Winston boarded his plane with a new perspective on life. He'd let things cool down for a while, get himself together then he really would take the first step and reach out to his brother. In the meantime, he prayed that he hadn't completely ruined his brother's or his sister-in-law's life.

DOUBLETAKE

Terrence and Tara

Tara raced into her sister's bedroom, concerned about why she hadn't answered the phone or the door. She'd called Sheridan to make sure he hadn't come home early. His concern escalated as well when he'd tried to call his wife and no one answered. Tara had driven like a mad woman across town, showing up at the house only moments before Terrence. Apparently Sheridan had called him, sending him to the house to check on Amira and the kids.

They'd found Nasir and his sister in his bedroom watching cartoons and picking cereal out of a box of Cheerios. Terrence went to check on the baby who'd obviously been crying his lungs out for quite some time. Under any other circumstances, Nasir probably would have gotten his baby brother but he was nowhere near tall enough to reach over the side of the crib. While Terrence checked on the little one Tara checked on Amira. She peeped into the bedroom; relieved to at least see her sister hadn't been kidnapped or worse. Now she just needed to find out why she hadn't gotten up to answer the phone or tend to the kids.

"Amira?" Tara shook her sister, trying to wake her. The pill bottle and alcohol on the nightstand were far from reassuring. "Amira, please wake up." She pulled the covers over her sister's body as she called out to Terrence.

He stood in the doorway, baby in hand. "What's wrong?"

"She won't wake up! She must have taken too many pills. We have to get her to the hospital!"

Amira stirred at the panic in her sister's voice. She fought the pull of the drugs and alcohol still pumping through her system. She tried to open her eyes but her lids felt like two lead paperweights.

"Amira? Amira, can you hear me?" Tara shook the groggy but more responsive Amira. She needed so much for her sister to be all right. What would she tell Sheridan and the kids? And how would she live with herself? She knew she should have stayed over while he was away.

"What..." Amira managed, lifting her hand, wanting to cover her eyes from the morning light but failing to have the strength to raise her palm more than a few inches above the bed.

"Amira, how many of these pills did you take?"

Her head rolled around on the pillow, the brown of her eyes peeping from beneath her eyelids only to disappear back behind the line of long lush lashes. Her body relaxed back into the bed as her mind once again slipped back beneath the spell of intoxicants.

"She looks to be all right. She just needs to sleep this off." Terrance placed a hand over Tara's shoulder. "Come on. Why don't you help me get the kids bathed and fed and we'll check on her a little later."

"But she's not fine. What if she took too many? What if she needs to have her stomach pumped or something?"

"She's been asleep all night. If she had taken too many it would have killed her by now. She shouldn't have mixed the two but she'll be fine once it wears off. Come on, I don't think dry Cheerios is the kind of breakfast the kids are used to and you know how this one gets when he doesn't get fed."

Terrance helped Tara up from the bed and led her out of the bedroom. They left Nasir and his sister to watch TV while they made breakfast. Tara moved around the kitchen gathering eggs, bacon, and grits while Terrance talked to Sheridan.

"Yeah man, the kids are fine. Amira mixed alcohol with sleeping pills." He played with the baby while Sheridan went on about how he'd warned her before about mixing the two. "It didn't look like she drank much but you know how little she is. Even a little bit of alcohol at her weight would have been enough to cause a reaction. We'll hang around until she's completely over this."

Terrence shared in his best friend's concern. The first time he's away for any length of time and his wife almost over doses. That was a big wakeup call.

"Don't worry. We'll make sure Amira and the kids are fine. Tara already said she's staying the rest of the week." After a pregnant pause, Terrance continued, "It's no big deal. You know y'all are family. I'll make sure Amira calls you once she's up."

Terrance watched Tara scramble the eggs and flip the bacon. When the oven dinged, she pulled the toast out and placed it on the stove. He finished his phone call with

Sheridan sliding the phone to the middle of the table. He secured the baby into the high chair, joining Tara in front of the stove.

"You almost done?" He leaned against the countertop watching as she scooped the eggs onto three of the four plates she'd laid out.

"Yep. You staying?" She stopped with the last bit of eggs in mid pour.

"I can't leave you here alone to take care of all of these kids and Amira. Besides, I haven't been spending enough time with my Godchildren. My sign language is getting a little rusty."

Tara poured the last bit of eggs on to the last plate. She poured grits on each plate and fill a bowl for the baby before turning to face Terrance. "Thanks for staying." She handed him the bowl to take to the table while she grabbed the plates.

"Not a problem. You want me to feed him?" Terrence tickled the little boy staring wide-eyed up at him under the chin.

"No, I got it. You mind getting Nasir and his sister?" She placed the two plates in her hand on the table with a spoon for baby girl and a fork for Nasir.

"Not at all."

Terrence corralled the little ones and herded them into the kitchen. With everyone situated at the table, and grace spoken over the food, they all dug in.

"You're not going to eat?" Terrance scooped a spoon full of mixed eggs and grits into his mouth. He'd watched the loving way she'd taken each spoonful of grits, blew on them to cool them before feeding them to the baby. It almost made him wonder why she didn't have any kids of her own.

"I put my plate in the microwave. I'll eat after junior here is done."

"Can I ask you something?" Curiosity got the best of Terrence. Tara was an attractive woman, career minded. She had so much going for her and yet he'd never heard her talk about a significant other or anyone special in her life.

"That all depends. Is this going to be a personal question?" She'd watched him making eyes at her.

She'd always thought of Terrence as a nice guy but she wasn't quite sure he was her type. He was a professional and she'd been impressed with the way his tailored-made suits fit him to the T. Still, he seemed a little too clean cut, way too much of a straight-line guy for her.

"It's kind of a personal question. Taking care of kids seems to come natural for you. I was just curious as to why you don't have any of your own." He bit into a piece of toast, cocking his head sideways as Nasir snickered. He wondered if the little boy had read his lips.

"Haven't found Mr. Right I guess. We were raised bridal shower before baby shower. I've still got plenty of time to start a family."

He caught a glimpse of sadness in her eyes as she turned away. "Can I ask you something else?"

"I guess."

"Would you ever consider having dinner with me?"

There, he'd put it out there. Sometimes Mr. Right was right in front of you; you just needed to open your eyes and see it for yourself.

"I don't know. Dating my brother-in-law's best friend might cause some conflict if things went sour."

"Come on, it's just dinner. No strings attached."

They both turned at the sound of Nasir sliding his chair across the floor as he pushed away from the table. He grabbed his empty plate and his sister's and placed them in sink. Grabbing his sister by the hand, he led her out of the room.

"What was that about?" Tara asked, scraping the last of the grits out of the bowl.

"Routine. Sheridan and Amira usually spend mornings talking. I guess Nasir sensed that this conversation was an 'adult' conversation so since they were finished, they're going to finish watching cartoons."

"Okay, that's creepy."

"Not really. Kids are smarter than most adults give them credit for." He stood, following suit, placing his plate on the stack with the others. "Now are you going to answer my question?" He walked over to the microwave, turning it on to heat up her food. On his way back across the kitchen, he took the empty grit's bowl and filled it with water, placing it on the pile of dishes.

"No strings attached?" She eyed him, wanting the truth.

"No string attached. What harm could it do?"

Tara considered his proposal. Dinner was no big deal.

People had dinner all the time. That didn't mean it was a date. And she'd get the opportunity to see if they really could have something. Maybe he could be the one. Maybe he'd been the one all along and she just hadn't taken the time to see it.

Tara reeled in her thoughts. One step at a time. "Sure. I'd love to have dinner with you."

"Then we'll work out the details once Sheridan is back. In the meantime," he moved across the kitchen, taking her plate from the microwave and placing it in front of her, "eat your breakfast while I get this one bathed." He scooped the baby from the high chair and exited the kitchen leaving Tara to finish her breakfast in peace.

DOUBLETAKE

Amira

Amira rolled over in bed covering her eyes with her arm. Man, she had a killer headache. She lay there trying to regain her bearings. There was too much light coming into the bedroom for it to be early morning and at the realization, she jerked up in bed. She grabbed her robe, dashing down the hallway concern for her children forcing her to ignore the cold floor and the sharp pain piercing her head with each step. It was too quiet in the house. She hadn't looked at the clock but something inside told her that the kids had probably been awake for hours now.

In such a hurry to check on her baby, Amira missed Tara sitting on the floor of the living room combing her baby girl's hair. Nasir lay napping on the couch so she wouldn't have seen him in her rush. Amira flung the door to the nursery open, expecting her baby to be balling his eyes out by now. Instead, she found him cradled in Terrence's arms, the both of them sound asleep in her gliding rocking chair. A sense of relief washing over her, Amira checked the other rooms searching for her oldest and baby girl. She knew Nasir would take care of his little sister. He'd been doing that a lot lately and she'd have to remember to do something really special for her little man to show her appreciation.

Not finding them in either of their bedrooms, Amira drudged her way back into the living room. The television was on; something she hadn't noticed in her scurry to make sure her baby was safe. She peeped over the back of the couch seeing Nasir curled up in the fetal position with his arms around a pillow.

She pulled the blanket up over his shoulders before speaking to Tara. "How long have I been out?"

"Huh?" Tara snapped around, her eyes growing big at the voice she hadn't expected. She grabbed her chest, taking in a couple of deep breaths hoping to slow down her now racing heart. "Don't do that."

"I'm sorry."

"You had us worried sick!"

Nasir stirred at his aunt's raised voice. He was mostly deaf but not completely and he was highly sensitive to vibration. Amira rubbed his back, soothing the child and enticing him to remain in his quiet slumber. When she was sure he again danced in dreamland, she sat down on the couch next to him.

"I guess I owe you and Terrance a thanks. I've been having a hard time sleeping since Sheridan left on Monday. I only took two pills." She laid her head on the back of the couch, closing her eyes as the throbbing intensified.

"But you mixed them with alcohol. You should have called me. I would have taken care of the kids while you got some rest."

"You know I can't sleep with people in the house."

"And what if something had happened to the kids? What if someone had broken in last night while you were dead to the world? What if there had been a fire?"

Tara's ranting only made Amira's head hurt worse. Her eyes started watering at the thought of what she'd done. Combined with the little drummer boy beating in her head, Amira was on the verge of breaking down. A tiny warm hand brushing away a tear made Amira open her eyes.

She pulled her oldest child into her arms, needing to give him a hug, her way of apologizing for risking his life. He returned her hug, laying his head on his mother's chest. Moments later, he pulled back, sitting up on her lap.

Daddy made sure we were safe last night. Nasir smiled up at his mother as he signed the words.

Baby, daddy is out of town.

No! He insisted, the peek between his eyebrows growing with each second. *I saw him. He came to see you and he tucked Kira in last night. I don't think he knows that I was awake but I saw him.*

Sliding her son back on the sofa Amira stood up and checked all of the locks on the windows and doors. When she returned she asked her sister, "Was the front door locked when you came in this morning?"

"As far as I know." She couldn't really say for sure. Terrence had opened the door. Tara tied the last ribbon on the end of the ponytail in the middle of baby girl's head before shifting to face her sister.

"Did anything look out of place?" Amira's eyes continued to peruse their surroundings, searching for any indication that someone other than her family and Terrence had been in the home.

"Not that I noticed. Why?"

"Nasir just said that he saw Sheridan last night in the house." Amira was glad her son had turned his attention to the television. She really didn't want him reading her lips or the concern on her face.

"That's impossible. I called him this morning to make sure he hadn't come home early when I couldn't get in touch with you. He was just as worried as I was. That's why he sent Terrence here to make sure everyone was safe."

"Maybe he was just dreaming?"

I was not! Nasir glared at his mother, crossing his little arms over his chest and bunching up his lips.

Damn. He must have turned around. *Okay baby. I believe you. You saw daddy last night.*

"You should call Sheridan. Terrence told him you'd call once you were up anyway. Don't worry. I'll watch over these two. Everybody's been fed and bathed so go make your call." Tara turned her attention back to the cartoon plastered across the fifty-two inch plasma screen television.

Making her way back to the bedroom Amira grabbed the cordless phone and dialed Sheridan's cell number. She tapped her foot, waiting for him to answer. She still hadn't looked at the clock and for a second she wondered if he was out at a site or in a meeting.

Prepared to leave a message, she was greeted instead by

a weary and worried "Are you okay?"

"Yeah baby. I'm fine. Sorry."

She listened as her husband's voice changed from concern with a tad bit of anger to relief. "No, the kids are fine. Terrence and the baby are sleeping in the nursery and Tara, Nasir, and your little demon are watching cartoons."

She rolled her eyes as her husband basically accused her of neglecting their children. "Hold on now." She cut off his ranting before he said something he'd regret. "This hasn't exactly been easy on me either." She paused as he slipped a few words in. "Taking care of the kids isn't my only responsibility. I do have a business to run you know and house work to do. Somebody around here has to make sure homework gets done, bodies get bathed and bellies get filled."

Amira stopped when she realized that Nasir was standing in the doorway of the bedroom watching her. "Look, your son is here. We'll finish this when you get back. I just called to let you know that I was fine and the kids were fine."

Amira pursed her lips as Sheridan continued to voice his opinion on how he didn't know how he was going to be able to keep this contract if every night he was up worried that something may have happened to his family.

Tired of hearing him fuss at her like she was his child instead of his partner Amira interrupted, "Look, did you come home last night?"

His reply of no was far from reassuring. She waited for him to ask the question she knew was coming.

"Nasir said he saw you last night. That you came to see

me and you tucked Kira."

Sheridan agreed with Amira that their oldest son must have been dreaming. He assured her that he'd talk to Nasir when he got back, which would be in another day or so. In the meantime, he made sure she understood that either Tara or Terrence was remaining at the house.

Finally, realizing that he wasn't going to let her off of the phone until she promised him that she'd make sure one of them was there, she gave in. "All right already. They can stay. But you need to hurry home. I miss you baby."

Amira couldn't hide the smile the words he spoke to her caused. He promised her that when he got back they'd catch up on all of the loving they'd been denied. The thought warmed her from the inside out, comforting her, making her believe that in the end all of this would work itself out.

She ended the call with a sense of love and comfort engulfing her.

Amira, Carmen, & Madison

Amira walked to the door of her bedroom, pushing the vacuum cleaner ahead of her. Things had gotten back to somewhat normal since Sheridan had returned. He'd said the trip went well and he'd even started coming home in the middle of the day to make sure she and their youngest child were doing well. She appreciated him trying to be there for her as much as possible. They'd made up when he came home and he'd promised her to spend more time with her so that when he did have to go out of town, she'd know that she was always on his mind.

Pushing the door closed, she cut off the vacuum cleaner as her eyes caught a glimpse of a white card near the foot of the table by the door. She leaned over, arm reaching around the nightstand to scoop the card from the tan carpet and flipping it over in her hand.

Amira grew pale, her legs growing weak as she stared at the female's name and phone number on the card. She flipped it over, the address of a local extended stay hotel staring back at her. She grabbed onto the wall, as her heart grew heavy. This couldn't be happening. Not now. It just couldn't be happening.

Her mind no longer focused on housework, Amira retreated to her backyard. She stared out into the vast landscaping for her manicured garden. She'd spent the last few minutes fighting to keep her eyes from glazing over. Even when she'd answered the door to let Madison and Carmen in she'd allowed the sadness to remain plastered on her face. Her friends had busied themselves with small talk, letting her wallow in her sorrow for a few minutes.

Carmen kept watching Amira, wondering why she seemed depressed. They'd come over to check on her, like they always did midweek, only to find her sitting out here staring out into space. She'd spoken with Tara to find out if anything had happened. The only thing Tara could think might be wrong with her sister was that Amira was still blaming herself for possibly endangering her children.

Carmen glanced over at Madison, wondering if they really should break the news to Amira while she was like this. Apparently, the woman already had plenty on her mind. But she needed to know. If anything, they'd promised to be upfront on stuff like this. They'd kept their mouths shut on the issue for far too long trying to devise a plan to break the news as gently as possible. Carmen was more than sure that the whole thing had been burning a hole in Madison's soul. That woman had never been able to keep a secret and this one was a doozey.

"Amira, we need to talk to you," Carmen started, waiting for the woman to turn in her direction.

"I'm not in the mood for this," Amira replied, her eyes closing as the tears threatened to escape.

"Well we don't exactly have good news. It's about Sheridan."

At the mention of her husband's name Amira looked up at her friend. She took in the worry in Carmen's eyes. She'd never seen her friend look so sad. Amira looked over at Madison who seemed to be content looking everywhere but at her. Did she have something to do with what Carmen wanted to tell her about Sheridan?

Amira started to worry. Sheridan had warned her about Madison. Had the woman finally crossed the line? Her hands formed fists as she focused her attention back on Carmen.

"I don't know how to tell you this but when Sheridan was supposed to be out of town, we saw some disturbing things."

"Disturbing things like what?" Slowly but surely anger started to replace the sadness in Amira's heart.

"Did you talk to Sheridan while he was gone?"

"What kind of question is that? Of course I talked to him, at least a couple of times a day every day."

"Did you talk to him in his hotel or from his cell phone?"

She hadn't thought about that. He'd given her his room number but every time she'd called he was out. She'd left messages and he'd returned them all. Now that she thought about it though, when he called back, he always called from his cell.

"His cell."

"Just tell her Carmen or I will." Madison replied, obviously tired of this back and forth questioning. She'd only agreed to let Carmen tell Amira because she was sure accusations would fly if she did.

"Look, the day we were at the mall, we saw somebody who looked a lot like Sheridan."

"When?" Amira glared at her friend, waiting for an answer.

"Before I answer that, let me finish. That wasn't the only time that we saw this. We also went to the movies and we saw him there too."

"What are you saying?" Doubts crept into Amira's mind. First she'd discovered the business card to a local hotel. Now her friends were trying to tell her that they'd seen Sheridan out with another woman.

Tired of Carmen dancing around this, Madison finally opened her mouth. "Sheridan was out with another woman; two other women to be exact. They were hugged up in the theatre, drooling all over each other. We followed them to a hotel and let's just say they weren't exactly being discreet."

"Madison!" Carmen was trying to be tactful but of course all of that came to an end with the blatant confession of her friend.

They both turned to look at Amira wondering when she was going to react. She just sat there, her eyes glazed over. Neither knew what to say. This had taken them all by surprise. Never in a million years would any of them have dreamed that Sheridan would do something like this. But they knew what they'd seen and neither had any other explanation.

Amira stood. She couldn't look at them. She needed to know and she knew where to find the answer to the question burning in her mind. Praying that this phone call would turn out for the best, Amira entered the quiet of her home.

She stared at numbers on the phone, building up the courage to do what she had to do. She took in a deep breath as she pressed the numbers one at a time. Her eyes drawn to the sun setting just outside of her bedroom window, Amira let the tears fall. Barely able to compose herself, she somehow formed to words. "I'm trying to verify some information." Amira asked the woman who answered the phone if they had a Sheridan Malcolm staying there during that week when her husband was supposed to be out of town.

Her heart grew heavy with each second that painstakingly ticked by. She kept telling herself that this wasn't happening. Her friends had to be mistaken. Her foot stopped in mid tap as the woman on the other line confirmed that they'd had a Sheridan Malcolm staying at the hotel the same week that Sheridan had gone on his business trip.

She hung up the phone, not taking the time to even say good-bye. This didn't make sense. How could he be in two places at once? With anger still racing through her veins, Amira dialed the handwritten number on the back of the business card. If the woman answered and she said she'd been with Sheridan, she didn't know what she'd do.

Her heart nearly stopped as someone answered the phone. Unfortunately it was a man who'd only recently gotten the number. A dead-end, at least for now. No closer to an explanation, Amira crawled into the bed. Why was this happening? She couldn't move, she couldn't think, all she could do was cry.

"Amira hun?" Madison tapped on the closed bedroom

door. They'd given her some time to let this all sink in, but when she still hadn't returned, they'd started to worry.

"Go away!" She didn't want to talk to anyone right not. Actually she did want to talk to one person but he wasn't around, as usual.

"We're not leaving until we know you're okay." Carmen leaned against the wall as Madison stood next to her staring at a closed door.

"I'm fine! Just leave me alone!" Amira buried her face in the pillow, not wanting them to hear her crying.

"We're just going to the other room. We'll watch the little one until Sheridan gets home."

Uh! Why did they have to mention his name? Amira wanted so much to call but what she was thinking needed to be said to his face. She lie there, numb, not knowing how she was going to deal with this. She had three kids to take care of and she wasn't sure she'd be able to do that on her own.

Sheridan took care of the major bills, the mortgage, lights, water, and gas. Most months he footed the nearly three hundred dollar a month grocery bill as well. She stopped, trying not to get ahead of herself. There had to be some other explanation and until she spoke with Sheridan, she'd hold on to the little hope she had of finding it.

Sheridan

S heridan rolled to a stop behind Madison's Benz that, as usual, was strategically placed in the middle of the turnaround of their driveway. He'd chewed her out before about blocking the garage. Then again, he was two hours early so he'd let it go this time.

His fingers tightened on the steering wheel as he huffed. All he wanted to do was take a steaming shower, grab a sandwich and plop down in front of the television. He'd tried to make it through the day but everything that could go wrong did. When he'd extinguished the last fire, metaphorically of course, he'd told his assistant that he was going home. He'd made it clear that unless one of the jobs literally went up in flames, anything anyone had a problem with could and would wait until tomorrow.

He climbed from the truck, making his way to the front door. He hoped Amira and her friends were out in the guesthouse or the gardens. He hadn't seen Madison or Carmen since he'd returned from his trip and the last people he wanted to deal with right now were those two. Actually, Carmen wasn't so bad. At least she carried herself in a respectful manor. Wish he could say the same about Madison.

Plastering as much of a smile as he could muster across his face, Sheridan entered his home. A man's home was supposed to be his castle but at this time of day he was sure it was more like a hen house. He closed the door, listening for any indication that the housewives had gathered for their little powwow. Silence. Maybe his day was looking up.

Heading in the direction of his bedroom, two pair of angry eyes boring into him caused Sheridan to stop. He took in the disgusting glares, first wondering why they were looking at him like he'd stolen Christmas and then wondering where Amira was. He stood there, waiting for one of them to say something, but the two women just continued to stare at him, shooting imaginary arrows in his direction, or so he assumed.

"Are you two just going to keep staring at me like I've just killed your best friend or are you going to tell me what the problem is?" Might as well get this over with, wasn't like this day could get much worse.

Carmen's eyes momentarily darted to Madison before she turned her attention back to Sheridan. This was Madison's department. She'd never quite mastered the art of telling people about themselves. Since Madison did it so well, Carmen thought it a shame to not let the maestro run free in her element.

"For the first time in my life, I do declare I'm at a loss for words." Madison shook her head, trying to form the words to put this man in his place.

Though Amira had been right about her vying for

Sheridan's attention, ultimately she never wished her friend harm. She'd never willingly ruin her friend's life. Not to say that if Sheridan left Amira, she wouldn't be the first one knocking on his door.

"You, without words? Oh this is going to be good." He shifted his weight to one foot, waiting for this little explanation of hers.

"Not good for you." She narrowed her eyes, a frown taking over her mouth.

"I don't have time for this." Sheridan turned, prepared to leave the two women sitting like crones waiting for death to come put them out of their misery.

"How could you cheat on a woman who'd give you the world?"

Snapping around, his face clearly indicated he didn't have the slightest idea what she was talking about. "What?"

"We saw you all hugged up with that hussie?" Madison refused to allow him to deny what he'd been doing. And after all that Amira did for him.

"What the hell are you talking about?"

"We almost didn't tell her but seeing you and that, I don't even have a name to call her, walking into that hotel. We couldn't just stand by and let her continue not knowing the truth."

"You know what?" That was it, snide remarks he could take, her eyeing him, no big deal, but he was not about to stand here and let some alcoholic, drug addict, adulterer accuse him of being unfaithful. "Get the fuck out of my house."

"I saw you too Sheridan," Carmen chimed in when she realized that he thought Madison was just trying to come between him and Amira.

"I don't give a damn what you two thought you saw. I have not, nor will I ever, cheat on my wife. Now get to stepping!"

With his hand pointing them to the door, Sheridan watched as Carmen placed his sleeping son in the playpen. The women grabbed their belongings, still staring at him like he was the scum beyond the bottom of a sewage pond. If they were coming at him with this, he could only imagine what they'd told Amira.

The accusers now expelled from his residence, Sheridan made sure his son was okay before he faced his wife. He was so sick of those two sticking their noses in his business. He'd let this slide for too long. From now on, he didn't want either of them in his home.

Sheridan crept into the bedroom, taking a seat on the side of the bed. He watched Amira sleep for a moment contemplating if he really wanted to wake her. She looked horrible, the residue of her tears staining her cheeks. Her friends had upset her, something that he refused to tolerate. He started to get up, deciding to let her come to him when she spoke.

"Why Sheridan? Why'd you have to go to somebody else? What was it that you weren't getting from me?" Her brows merged into a worried peak in the center of her forehead. She'd spent the last hour trying to figure out where she'd gone wrong.

"Amira baby, I don't know what your friends told you but I did not cheat on you." He said the words in a calm voice as he rubbed his hand up and down her back. She trembled beneath his touch and he wondered if the reaction was caused by fear or desire.

She jerked away her expression changing to disbelief. "Don't lie to me." She held the card out to him before saying, "I called the hotel. They had you staying there when you were supposed to be on your business trip. Was that other woman the real business you were tending to?"

He took the card from her, studying the hotel address. He'd never been to this place in his life. Besides, it was a little low class for his tastes. Still, he wondered how someone could have stayed in a hotel under his name.

Sheridan picked up the phone and dialed the number to the hotel. He spoke with the same woman Amira had talked to and again she confirmed that someone had used his information to stay in the hotel. Hanging up the phone, Sheridan tried to make sense of all of this.

"I don't know how someone got ahold of my information but I assure you Amira, I went on my trip." Sheridan had his suspicions but he wouldn't be able to confirm anything until he had things squared away with his family.

"How can I believe you? My friends are telling me they saw you with other women and then the reservations and hotel stay. I don't know what's true and what's not." She pulled her knees up to her chest, wrapping her arms around them. Her eyes focused on her husband who seemed to be just as much at a loss as she was.

"If you want me to call my client, then I will. You can talk to the man. Not only that," he left her there for a moment making his way into the sitting room attached to their bedroom. He kept most of his business paperwork in the makeshift office. Returning, he handed her the boarding passes for the two additional flights they'd taken. "Look at the passes 'Mira, I got on those planes."

"Then how?" This didn't make sense.

"Shh." He placed a finger over her lips before she said another word. "I don't know, but I intend to find out. Look, go back to sleep. I'll watch over our little ones, okay?"

Still not sure if she believed him, Amira crawled under the covers. Crying had taken a lot out of her so she welcomed the time to herself. "Okay."

Her lips brushed against his before he got up to let her rest. Closing the bedroom door, Sheridan walked into the living room scooping his still sleeping son into his arms. He'd almost lost his family and he needed to have his little man close as a reminder of how good he really had it.

Sheridan picked up the phone and dialed his mother. There were too many coincidences for him not to be a little suspicious. Though he was sure this was just a case of mistaken identity and fraud, he needed to be sure. Talking with his father for a few minutes Sheridan finally got his mother on the phone. She'd have what he needed to get in contact with his brother. At least, that's what he hoped.

Winston and Jasmine

Winston checked the caller id trying to figure out who'd be calling at this hour, not that he didn't already know. For the past few weeks, he'd been avoiding Sheridan's calls. He actually wished his brother would go away.

Glancing up from the computer screen just as Jasmine reached for the phone, he shouted, "Don't answer that."

Her hand hovered over the lit up contraption as Winston stopped her. "Why?"

Thinking fast, he replied, "That's my mamma and I don't feel like hearing her mouth."

As the phone stopped ringing, Jasmine eyed her man. "Why don't you want to talk to your mother?"

"I just don't, okay," he snapped, his attention drawn back to the website he'd been playing on. She was starting to work his nerves. He was trying to remain civil, but if she continued cackling, he was going to go off.

Jasmine looked over the man who, day by day, grew more distant. She didn't exactly believe him. Since he'd returned from his trip, he'd changed. She couldn't quite put her finger on it, but something about her man was different. Even when they made love it was like his mind was somewhere else.

She pulled up a chair watching as he started a new game of chess with an online opponent. "Winston, we need to talk."

Though she couldn't see it, he rolled his eyes. Here it comes. He clicked the "X" on his screen closing off his game to give Jasmine his undivided attention. He wasn't really going to pay attention to her but he'd at least make an effort to look convincing.

"So what do you want to talk about?" He locked his fingers, resting his hands on his stomach. Noticing the bulge, he made a mental note to start working out again.

"I don't like the Winston you've become."

"Huh?"

"Since you came back, you've changed. And not necessarily for the better."

"I don't know what you're talking about?"

"You know exactly what I'm talking about." She stopped as she heard her voice rise. This wasn't exactly how she wanted to confront him. Jasmine drew in a deep breath, holding it before allowing the air to escape through her parted lips. "I don't want to argue with you; I just want to know what's going on. Since you got back, you won't talk to me. I feel alienated in my own home and I don't know what to do about it."

Her eyes begged for his reassurance. She wanted

things to go back to how they were. She needed to know what had happened while he was in Atlanta.

"What do you want me to do Jasmine?" He threw his hands up, trying his best not to just get up and walk away. She was pushing, and the last thing he needed right now was someone else pushing.

She looked him square in the eyes when she said the words. "I want you to tell me why you've shut me out?"

"Damnit woman, I don't know."

"What do you mean, you don't know?"

"I've got so much on my mind and I don't know how much longer I can deal with this shit?"

"Talk to me Winston." It wasn't like she was asking him to make a lifelong commitment, though lately that had been on her mind. She just wanted to be there for her man. "I just might be able to help."

"Look, some shit just don't feel right."

That was a start. When she realized he wasn't going to continue, she asked, "What doesn't feel right?"

"I don't know how to explain it. In case you haven't noticed, I haven't exactly been sleeping."

She had noticed that he was spending more than his fair share of nights pacing in the computer room of their home. She'd noticed some other changes in her man that were disturbing, changes that had led her to make a stop at the drug store for a home pregnancy test.

"I need to ask you something Winston." Jasmine lifted

her weight from the chair and crossed the room. She was about to accuse him of something and she didn't want to be in reaching distance. She faced him, giving him that much respect.

"Did something happen while you were in Atlanta that I need to know about?"

"Like what?"

"Don't act dumb. When's the last time you got up in the middle of the night for White Castles?" Jasmine winced as a pain pierced her heart. His behavior had been the same when she was pregnant. Unfortunately, she'd lost the baby. "I'm coming at you like a real woman and I'm asking you straight up, did you screw around and get somebody pregnant?"

Winston bit his tongue. He couldn't stand to see the hurt in her eyes but she had no right to accuse him of anything. She didn't know what he'd been through and this wasn't helping one bit. He stared at her with angry eyes. "You know what? I don't need this shit!" He glared at her before grabbing his keys and walking out. If he stayed there one moment more, he was going to hurt her.

Jasmine stood in the office, the tears starting to fall. Her legs gave way when the walls shook. She was more than sure the sound of the front door slamming had probably woken their neighbors. She still didn't have an answer so she didn't know what to believe. All signs pointed to someone being pregnant, but she knew for a fact that she wasn't that someone.

Pulling her knees up to her chest and burying her face in her folded arms, Jasmine sat on the floor of the office and cried her heart out. She loved that man so much and yet, in this very moment, that love was tearing her heart apart.

Amira and Sheridan

S heridan reached over, patting the nightstand in search of snooze button on the blaring alarm clock. He pressed the button, his hand resting on top of the clock still too tired to slide it back beneath the covers. He laid there, his mind still halfway between dreamland and reality. A warm presence at his side and an arm draped over his stomach drew his attention. He opened his eyes enough to realize that Amira still lay in the bed beside him. He glanced at the clock, making sure he'd set it for the right time. Seven a.m.

He considered waking her then decided that the least he could do was let her sleep. She did so much for him and the kids and since Mother Nature had seen fit to allow her some extra Z's, then he'd let her get them. He wiggled his way from the bed, careful not to wake his sleeping beauty. Standing at the side of the bed, he watched her, her chest moving up and down, as she remained trapped in a peaceful slumber. He pulled the covers over her nude body and slipped out the door to get the kids up.

With Nasir getting his little sister dressed and the baby changed and sitting in the high chair at the kitchen table, Sheridan busied himself preparing breakfast. He was glad he'd convinced Amira to start buying canned biscuits. He loved her homemade ones, but on a morning like this, he was glad to just be able to open a package and slide the bread in the oven.

"Need some help?" Amira stood in the doorway watching her husband scramble eggs and flip bologna with ease. She didn't know why the last few weeks since he'd gotten back from his trip she'd been so tired.

"No. I think I can handle it." He glanced over his shoulder watching as his wife rested her head on the doorframe and closed her eyes. "Amira…"

"Huh?"

"Come here baby. I need to talk to you about something." Sheridan turned off the bologna and scraped the eggs into the bowl. He slid the pan of biscuits out of the oven and buttered them before sliding them on the plate.

Amira leaned on the counter, watching as her husband drained the last piece of bologna and placed it on a plate.

"You all right?" He glimpsed her from the corner of his eye. The corners of her mouth turned down and she still had sleep in her eyes.

"Yeah. Just tired." She placed her elbows on the countertop, adjusting her weight so that she got into a comfortable position.

"That's what I wanted to talk to you about." Sheridan was pretty sure he knew what was going on with his wife. He'd been anticipating his cravings to start but to date he hadn't had any. "You been kinda slow this week and I saw you with marshmallows the other day. And the raw spaghetti."

"So?"

"So," He faced her, pulling her into his arms so that her back was to him. He encircled her waist, his hands resting on her stomach. "You sure we don't have another delivery on the way?"

The night he'd come back from his business trip, they'd more than made up for the lost week. They'd gotten so caught up with each other that they hadn't used any protection. For him, another child was no big deal. For Amira though, it meant another warm body to tend to. She'd finally gotten their youngest potty nearly trained, he was picking it up quickly to be so young, and if she were pregnant, they'd be starting all over again.

"Actually, I've been thinking the same thing. I have been craving lately and I'm late but I thought it could just be the stress of you working extra hours and being here alone. We'll know for sure when breakfast is over."

"How's that?" He nuzzled her neck, trailing kisses from her ear to her shoulder. She'd only put on a robe that left her nude beneath that.

"I took a pregnancy test before I came out."

She laid her head against his chest wrapping her fingers around his. All sorts of thoughts ran through her mind. She loved her children. She loved her husband just as much. But if she were pregnant, she'd be back to changing diapers, cleaning up baby drool and breast-feeding. And just when she was getting use to not having to deal with most of those things.

"Guess I'm going to have to get you some help around here." He twirled her around, gazing into her eyes before brushing her lips with his.

The squeals from their daughter coming closer indicated that their older children would be here any minute now. "Come on, let's get this food on the table." Amira pushed away and Sheridan allowed her to put some space between them.

He grabbed the bowl of eggs and plate with the bologna while Amira carried the biscuits to the table. They each took their seats and dug in. Unlike most mornings, Sheridan spent less time talking with his son and more time staring at his wife.

Whether she believed it or not, he was more that sure that she was pregnant. She didn't look happy and for the first time Sheridan wondered if she'd be all right with another child. He'd wait until they knew for sure before talking to her about it.

An anxiety hung in the air the entire meal, the source, Amira. She tried not to think about it, to concentrate on feeding her son, but her mind kept drifting back to the test. She watched the clock, which seemed to have stopped. These few minutes were turning out to feel like a few hours.

"You going to look?" Sheridan asked, standing up and taking his empty plate to the sink. His son followed suit, handing his and his sister's plates to his father. Nasir helped his sister from her chair and with her hand in his; they trotted out of the kitchen.

"Your son knows something is up." Amira scraped the

last spoonful of eggs from the bowl and held it out to their youngest child. She'd watched Nasir's eyes dart back and forth from her to his father.

"I'll go talk to him. Come get me before you look." He pecked her on the cheek before leaving the kitchen.

Halfway through the living room thoughts of his brother darted into Sheridan's mind. It stopped him causing his brow to draw together. He looked around the room not quite knowing what triggered the thoughts. He had the strange feeling that he was being watched. He'd had a similar feeling the week before he'd gone on his business trip.

Sheridan walked over to the window, peeping through the blinds only to see the street empty as usual. He faced the kitchen again thinking maybe Amira had been watching him. Maybe it was just in his head. He shook the feeling, crossing back to the other side of the room and heading down to his son's room.

He stuck his head in the door, expecting Nasir to be sitting on the bed watching cartoons and waiting for him to indicate it was time for them to go. Instead he found his son's book bag on the bed waiting with no Nasir. Sheridan continued down the hall to his daughter's room. He found Nasir packing his sister's bag while she played with one of her dolls.

He knelt beside the little boy, placing his hand on Nasir's arm to get his attention. *Well, aren't you just the helpful little man.*

Is mommy okay? He signed back, staring into his father's eyes with a look of sadness.

Mommy has had a lot to do taking care of all of us. I am sure she is thankful for your help. We both do.

I want old mommy back. Nasir's eyebrows rose, showing his concern for his mother's wellbeing.

Sheridan smiled at his son. He was growing up, a little faster than Sheridan wanted but not too unexpected. He'd been overly observant as an infant and with as quickly as he'd picked up sign language Sheridan knew his little man was special.

Daddy will make sure mommy gets rest so she will be back to her old self. Sheridan faced the door as his son's eyes lifted over his shoulder. Seeing Amira in the doorway with the baby on her hip he turned back to his son. *Finish helping your sister and we'll leave in a minute.* He gave the boy a hug before joining his wife at the door.

"You ready?" Sheridan grabbed the little boy from his wife following her down the hall toward their bedroom.

"The sooner I know for sure, the better."

"Babe," he placed a hand on her arm stopping her before she opened the door, "I meant what I said. If you need some help, I can get you some help."

"I appreciate that." She pushed open the door, heading into the bathroom while her husband sat on their bed playing with their son.

She was only gone a moment. She sat down beside her husband, a blank expression on her face. Her head hung down and her hands were cradled between her legs.

"Amira?" Sheridan laid the baby in the center of the bed. He propped one leg up on the side and covered her hands with his.

"Guess it's a good thing you got that contract, looks like we have another mouth to feed."

Sheridan didn't know how to take her solemn expression. She'd been happy when she'd found out she was pregnant before so he wondered why she seemed so down this time.

"What's wrong? I thought you'd be happy. We always said we wanted a house full of kids." He placed his hands over hers offering what little comfort he could.

"I know, but I thought it was going to be us. With this new contract and you traveling all the time, it's becoming more of me than us."

Sheridan took in a deep breath. He knew his new work hours were going to put a strain on their marriage. With this new baby though, he got the feeling that Amira might hit her breaking point.

"Look," he dug into his pocket, pulling a credit card from his wallet. "Call your sister and you two go to the spa."

"What about the baby?" Amira reached out to her son, pulling his t-shirt down over his belly.

"I'll drop him off at daycare with baby girl. Relax. Get some rest. I'll come home early and we'll talk about all of this. We'll figure something out. I promise."

As Sheridan stood, he picked up the squirming little boy, propping him in the bend of his elbow. "Are you going to make a doctor's appointment?"

"Yeah."

"I mean it 'Mira, get some rest. I'll see you this afternoon."

Though he wanted to remain by his wife's side, getting out of work today was impossible. He'd get what he needed to get done as quickly as possible and be home before she knew it.

He'd have to explain to Nasir that there'd be a new addition to their family. But he was more than sure his growing little man would understand. Baby girl would be a different story. He'd figure something to tell her sooner or later.

Amira and Tara

Amira relaxed as the masseuse placed each of the five hot stones on her back. She emptied her mind, allowing the scent of lavender and the soft music to drown out the worry. The heat lulled the tension in her back and shoulders, allowing her to experience total relaxation.

It hadn't taken much to convince her sister to ditch work and come get her. She'd basically told Tara that Sheridan had taken all of the kids and that he'd given her a credit card to get a massage. Tara never turned down an offer for pampering so, within the hour, they'd found themselves submerged in a soothing atmosphere without a care in the world.

"So, are you going to tell me what's the occasion for this day away from the children?" Tara had kept her question to herself during the ride over and through their facials. She hoped Amira would tell her on her own. No such luck.

"Do I have to?" She enjoyed the feel of large warm

hands kneading her back and shoulders.

"You don't have to but something must really be up for Sheridan to have taken all of the kids. The last time you got a spa day in the middle of the week you were…" Tara caught herself before she finished her sentence. Was it possible?

"I was wondering how long it was going to take you to figure it out."

"Again Amira? You trying to make this an annual event?" The firm hands on her back kept Tara from getting up and glaring at her sister.

"No. I'm not even sure how I feel about having another baby?"

She hoped her sister understood where all of this was coming from. One minute she wanted this child, the next she wasn't sure. For once, she envied Tara. At the drop of a hat she could sail away to another country and explore the world. She and Sheridan had enough money to do the same, except she'd be worried sick if Nasir's baby sitter knew sign language or if baby girl had her asthma medicine and that youngest one, the list went on and on with his needs.

"You're not thinking of not having this child, are you?" Tara never thought she'd be asking that question. Her sister loved children. Always had and always would. And yet, she heard a bit of something in Amira's voice that concerned her.

"That's not an option and you know it. Sheridan would have a fit." Amira huffed at the mere suggestion of her not keep this baby. Whether she liked it or not, she was going to have another child to tend to.

"There are other options, you know. How are you going to handle four kids?"

"The same way I handled three. Besides, Sheridan offered to get me some help around the house. If I can get someone to do the cleaning and the laundry, I should be fine." Amira winced as her masseuse pulled back on her shoulder. After a moment of stretching she felt the muscle loosening.

"Well you know you always have me. If you ever need anything…" Tara thought Amira sounded stressed already. Not good for the baby.

More than anything, Tara wanted her sister to be happy. In the end though, she wanted Amira to be realistic. If there was something on her mind concerning this addition to her ever-growing family, Tara thought it best to get the issue out in the open now before it had any adverse effect on her sister's marriage or family.

"I know, I know. Hey, speaking of children, how come you haven't settled down and had a couple?" Amira tried to steer the conversation in another direction. She'd come to the spa to relax and talking about her current dilemma wasn't exactly relaxing.

"I've been thinking about that lately." Tara quieted down, slipping into deep contemplation. The longer she remained single, the more she enjoyed her freedom. She loved spending time with her niece and nephews and many nights she wondered what her life would be like with the pitter-patter of little feet running through her house but she wasn't sure about having a family of her own.

"Tara?"

Where to start? As far as Tara was concerned, her sister always had the perfect life, not a care in the world. Tara never thought of her life panning out the way Amira's did. That worked for some people, but she wasn't sure it would work for her.

"You know, marriage isn't for everyone," Tara started, not sure she wanted to have this conversation with Amira right now, especially with her having another date with Terrence tonight. They'd decided to keep their dating under wraps until they knew for sure that whatever this thing was they had was going somewhere. Tara had to admit to herself that it was nice to have someone to cuddle and hang out with.

"I know that," Amira finally replied. "You don't have to be married to have a family you know. You're an adult, capable of making your own decisions. Hey, remember when we were little and we used to talk about when we grew up, we wanted all of these babies?"

"Yeah. And you always had this picture perfect prince charming to provide for you." Tara snickered, remembering them as little kids sitting around the dining room table at their make believe tea parties planning their futures.

"I don't recall you ever saying anything about a prince charming."

"I can't believe you actually remember that." Sometimes Amira surprised her with the little things she remembered. Tara never thought that the little things meant so much but every time her sister reminded her of their childhood, she realized how much those minute details had stuck with them both.

"I remember a lot of things. You could adopt. There

are plenty of children out there that would love to have a home. You'd have to cut back on your hours though. Not that I think that would be a problem for you."

"I've considered that but I want my children, even if they are adopted to have a male role model. I'm not saying that I want a husband but every child needs to see how a real man treats a real woman."

"Well, what about Sheridan? I mean, I'm sure that your kids would be spending plenty of time with our kids and Sheridan would be a wonderful influence on them." Amira released a moan as her masseuse pulled back on her shoulder, again making sure any tension left dissipated. One thing she'd learned over the years of being pampered, she kept all of her tension in her neck and shoulders which was a bad thing when you were carrying around an eighteen-month-old child most of the day.

She really needed to talk to Sheridan about that. Unlike their other children, their youngest son hadn't started walking until he was sixteen months. They were probably to blame for that. She carried him around most of the time and then passed him off to his daddy when he got home. That boy spent so little time on the floor that he really didn't have a reason to learn to walk.

"It's not just that. Raising kids is hard work and a lifetime commitment. I don't know if I can handle it alone."

Tara had thought about having a child on her own, no string attached for the father. She'd even talked with a few of her male friends who'd been more than willing to be donors. They'd even asked to remain a part of the child's life if she'd allow it. But she still had so many unanswered questions that she continued to delay her decision on the matter.

"Well, you know I'll need some help with the new baby."

"So you want me to take a trial run, huh?" Tara's masseuse indicated that she should turn over. She did. Lying on her back she could see Amira as she rolled over to her side and eventually onto her back.

"I'm not going to be much help the first few weeks after delivery. Usually Sheridan takes duty outside of feedings. Considering his new schedule though, I could use a few helping hands. I don't mind hiring someone to help with the housework but I'm not comfortable with the idea of a nanny. Children need their family, their real family."

"You know I'm here if you need me. Just give me a heads up and I'll take a month or so off of work to be at your beck and call."

"At least someone will be," Amira said under her breath.

Tara was sure that her sister hadn't meant for her to hear the comment. Needless to say, she heard every word. "It really bothers you that Sheridan might not be able to be there for you with this baby, doesn't it?"

"I don't really know. I'm used to him being here when I need him. I just feel like I'm going to have to do this alone."

"Have you talked to him about this?"

"We haven't had the chance to talk. I just found out this morning. We're supposed to talk tonight when he gets home from work."

"Are you going to tell him how you feel?"

"I haven't figured that out yet. I don't want to seem needy."

"Asking for help is not being needy. If this is bothering you enough for you to be questioning whether or not you can handle another child, then you need to tell Sheridan that. It takes two to make things work Amira. He's offering help; take him up on the offer."

"I'll think about it. I'm not making any promises though."

The two women laid in silence as their masseuses completed their massages. Amira took the time to really think about what her sister said. She made some decisions, hoping that Sheridan would understand and compromise on what it was she needed.

DOUBLETAKE

Amira and Sheridan

With her head resting against her husband's shoulder, Amira closed her eyes. It seemed like only yesterday that they'd been in this doctor's office checking on the progress of their youngest son. She'd hoped to not be sitting in this hard chair in the yellow pastel room with mothers rocking crying infants, toddlers banging toys against the plastic table and chairs in the corner, and snotty nosed preschoolers sucking their thumbs. The longer they sat, there the more she dreaded going through this again.

"You all right babe?" Sheridan laid his arm around her shoulders. He'd been staring at her as her emotions played across her face.

She wrapped her arms around her stomach, her head drooping down. She couldn't allow him to see the confusion in her eyes. She'd been grappling with the realization of being pregnant for almost three weeks now and each day it seemed more real. Not feeling like she had much control over the situation, she'd tried to accept it and be happy. Unfortunately she hadn't been able to convince herself of her joy.

Sheridan's fingers beneath her chin raising her face up to look at him made Amira opened her eyes. Her eyes glazed over as she fought to control her emotions. Looking at the joy beneath her husband's worried eyes, she couldn't bring herself to crush his hopes for her and this baby.

"Talk to me Amira. Please." Seeing her like this was nearly tearing him apart. He'd watched her go through so much over the past few days but every time he asked if she was okay, she'd unconvincingly say yes.

His thumb brushed across her cheek as she lost the battle with her tears. He cradled his wife's face in his palms, wishing she'd just open up. She'd never shut him out like this and he didn't have a clue as to what might be causing her such distress.

"Amira Malcolm."

Secretly thanking God for the interruption, Amira grabbed her purse and the notebook with her and her children's medical histories in it. She allowed her husband to help her up and with his fingers wrapped around her elbow, she let him guide her in the direction of the nurse standing in the door.

Sheridan stood to the side while the nurse took Amira's blood pressure and temperature. He didn't like the fact that her blood pressure was a little elevated. He was sure whatever she had on her mind was a contributing factor.

With height, weight, pressure and temperature checked, the couple followed the nurse down a hall of doors until she stopped in front of the only open door. Sheridan waited outside of the room for Amira to change into the gown. She'd been covering up a lot more lately so when she'd asked for a moment he allowed her the space. When she cracked the door, he entered, taking a seat in the chair next to the table. He intertwined his fingers with hers observing the sadness still lingering in her eyes.

"I need to ask you something babe." He sat there, staring at her, waiting for her to really see him. Her eyes locked with his and he understood her silent reply. "Do you want this baby?"

Though it pained him to ask her the question, he'd eliminated any other concerns. They discussed how they were going to handle his working and her needs during the pregnancy as well as after the baby was born. They'd worked out, as much as possible, the whole thing with Madison and Carmen and the accusations, or at least he'd thought they had. The only thing he could think of was that she had a problem with this pregnancy.

Amira continued to stare at him, not able to bring herself to tell him the truth. If she told him she wasn't sure that she wanted to have this child she didn't know what he'd do. But he'd asked the question for a reason.

"I want the truth Amira. Do you want this baby?"

Focusing on a spot over his shoulder to keep from breaking down, she managed to reply, "I don't know."

He squeezed her hand, his gaze remaining on her. He'd suspected as much but it hadn't really hit home until she'd just said the words. He didn't know what to think. Right now he was just in limbo, torn between a life he'd helped create and his wife's sanity. Sheridan had watched her change over the few weeks of this pregnancy and her sullenness wasn't good for the baby. If she really felt that she didn't want this child, then they had a lot to talk about once this visit was over.

Their heads turned at the sound of a knock at the door.

"Can you make it through this visit?" Sheridan's eyes darted back to his wife.

She nodded, hoping her response was the truth.

The doctor slipped into the room, taking a seat on the side of the bed opposite Sheridan. The woman looked over her patient, noting the slumped shoulders and red eyes.

"Did I interrupt something?"

Amira glanced at Sheridan, as if asking permission to answer the doctor's question. "No," she finally said.

"So," the doctor took one last look at the couple, not convinced she hadn't interrupted something, before getting back to business. Logging into the computer, she quickly reviewed the information entered by the nurse. "I see the Malcolm family is going to have another addition."

Amira gave the woman a weak smile but chose not to comment. She focused on the round face of her doctor realizing that the woman had gained a little weight since the last time she'd been in.

"Your last period was September 15th? Is that correct?"

"Yes," Amira responded.

"That would make the date of conception around, September 28th."

Sheridan raised an eyebrow at the doctor's comment as he watched her type in the additional information into the computer. September 28th couldn't be right. He was out of town on the twenty-eighth of September and the days before and after it.

As much as he wanted to say something, Amira was already grappling with so much. Sheridan knew that dates of conception were only estimates, and with Amira still not regular since their last child, it was possible that the date was off by a couple of days.

Sheridan gave the women some privacy to perform the physical exam. He started to worry when they were in there for longer than usual but when the doctor opened the door and stepped out, he slipped in to check on his wife.

"So is everything all right." He grabbed the sweater from the chair, handing it to his wife.

"Yeah. We have to go downstairs for the blood work and ultra sound." She slid the sweater over her head, pulling it down over her bare breasts.

When she reached for her coat, Sheridan wrapped his hands around her waist. She looked up at him, still fighting back tears. He saw the need in her eyes and he offered his strength in the form of a hug.

"We'll get through this baby. I promise you. Everything is going to be just fine." He rocked her in his arms for a moment, giving her some time to calm down. When she pulled away, they gathered the rest of her belongings and exited the room headed down the stairs to finish her tests.

DOUBLETAKE

Sheridan

Sheridan cringed at the sound of the basketball echoing through the enclosed gym. He dribbled his way down the court half concentrating on the ball as it bounced against the floor then returned to his hand. He reached the three-point line on the far end of the court, Terrence blocking his shot, reaching, trying to knock the ball away.

Slipping back into his daydream, Terrence batted the ball from his Sheridan's hand. Making his way down the court, he made a quick lay-up and turned. To his surprise, Sheridan still stood at the three-point line on the other side, seemingly staring out into nothing.

"Sheridan!" A little disturbed at his best friends preoccupation with something, Terrence jogged back to where Sheridan stood.

"Yeah?" Sheridan blinked, realizing that he no longer had the ball. He glanced in Terrence's direction before heading over to the bench. He sat down, grabbing a towel to wipe away the streams of sweat trailing down his face.

They'd been playing one on one for nearly an hour. The only reason Sheridan had agreed to come was that he needed some time away from Amira. He had a lot on his mind: his brother, his wife, and his business. Things were starting to get to him so he'd hoped that a little exercise would help ease his mind. Oh, how wrong he'd been.

Terrence wrapped a towel around his shoulders as he sat down on the bench next to his boy. "I haven't beaten you this bad in a long time. What's going on man?"

Sheridan guzzled down the remainder of his sports drink before leaning forward with his elbows resting on his knees. He stared out into the darkening sky. It'd be night soon and though he wasn't really ready to, he needed to be getting home soon.

"I got a question?" Sheridan said, leaning back on the bench and locking his fingers behind his head. He only held the pose for a moment before he got a whiff of himself. He'd have to head straight for the shower as soon as he was home.

"Sup?"

"When I was out of town, how was Amira?" Sheridan tilted his head back, wiping away the beads of sweat running down his face.

"What do you mean by how was she?"

"Like, was she acting nervous?"

"No. Why?" Terrence didn't like the direction this conversation was going. Since he'd returned and especially since he'd found out that Amira was pregnant, Sheridan had withdrawn, almost shutting her out at times.

Sheridan had thought about this for a few weeks now. Maybe he was just being paranoid. He needed to talk to someone before he just flat out accused his wife of something. Hopefully, bouncing some ideas off of Terrence would shed some light on the situation.

"What about the day you and Tara showed up at the house when we couldn't get in touch with her. Did anything look out of place?"

"No." He hadn't meant to say the word so fast. One thing he hadn't mentioned to Tara or Sheridan was that the lock on the storm door was unlocked. He hadn't really thought anything of it, considering the deadbolt and handle look on the front door had been secured. Now though, he wondered.

Terrence narrowed his gaze at his friend, "What are you getting at Sheridan?"

"I don't know man. I just got this feeling, ya know?" Sheridan tossed the ball at a couple of guys who'd just walked onto the court. He was way done for the day. This little exercise excursion hadn't done a thing for him.

"No I don't. What kind of a feeling?"

"Like some shit ain't right. You know, since we found out Amira was pregnant; I've been waiting for my cravings to start. I got them just as bad as she did with all of the other kids. Something just seems different about this one." A lot of things seemed different about this one, but he'd keep that to himself.

"Okay Sheridan. You straight trippin'." Terrence shook his head, not believing that the perfect couple could be having problems.

"I ain't trippin' man." Sheridan frowned at his friend before turning his attention back to the courts. "It's been a lot of bullshit."

"Bullshit like what?"

"You can't say anything to Amira but I actually believe Nasir when he said he saw somebody that night." Sheridan grabbed his towel, draping it over his head.

"Here we go. I though you cleared that up. He was dreaming." They'd had this discussion. Why was Sheridan bringing it up again?

"Naw man, hear me out. Nobody, not even a kid's dreams are that vivid. He described this man's features in detail. Don't get me wrong, I thought about the fact that his description was close to me. Still the fact that he'd tucked baby girl back into bed. No kid's going to make that up." Crossing his hands over his stomach, Sheridan continued, "And it isn't just that. I haven't said anything to her but when the doctor gave us the estimated date of conception and her due date, I started thinking. If my math is right, then she got pregnant around the same time I headed out on my business trip."

"Hell man, you know you got her pregnant. I do recall the two of you excusing yourselves from the table the day you headed out. Me and Tara may not have said anything but we ain't stupid."

"True. But it's close man, the days are just not adding up to me." Sheridan didn't want to feel this way. He wanted to believe that his wife was faithful, but every time he thought about that baby, that nagging feeling inside returned. His gut was telling him that the child Amira carried wasn't his.

"Man, get that shit out of your head. Amira did not cheat on you."

"I wish I was as sure. Everything about this pregnancy feels wrong to me. I don't feel the closeness to her that I normally do when she's pregnant. Sometimes I can't even stand to be in the same room with her."

"Give it some time. This pregnancy has been hard on the both of you. You two just need some time to adjust. I think the stress of your new work situation has you both on edge. And you know her hormones are way out of whack."

"I guess you're right. Maybe we both just need some space." Sheridan grabbed his bag. Bidding his friend goodnight, he walked to the other side of the courts and out the door, heading home to his wife and kids.

DOUBLETAKE

Amira

Amira rolled over onto her side again, trying to get comfortable. She'd tossed and turned most of the night, trying to ward off the aching in her back. Realizing that the position she'd just adjusted to only made the pressure worse, she crawled out of bed. Sheridan still had to get up in the morning to go to work and she didn't want to wake him so she snuck out of the bedroom in search of some relief.

With one hand on the wall to guide her down the hallway leading from their bedroom to the kitchen and her other hand rubbing circles on her stomach trying to soothe her baby, Amira retreated into the kitchen to make some chamomile tea. She filled the top of the coffeemaker with water and pressed the button to heat the water.

Waiting for the water to boil, Amira reached into a cabinet above the sink to grab the tea. Immediately she knew that was a mistake. A sharp pain in her side caused her to wrap her fingers around the counter in an attempt to ward off the pain. She bore the pain as much as she could without being too loud. She'd had backaches before with their daughter, making her believe that this child was a girl as well. Both she and her husband wanted this child to be a surprise, so they'd opted not to know the sex of the baby until he or she was born.

Breathing her way through the pain, Amira grabbed the step stool and grabbed the tea. As she heard the last of the water in the coffeemaker come to a boil, she headed to the other side of the kitchen rubbing her swollen belly with each step. She reached for the pot, sliding it from the maker to pour the water over the tea. But she never made it back to the island where she'd placed her cup.

She dropped the pot, the hot water and glass littering the floor. Amira screamed, her fingers again tightening on the counter as she felt another contraction. Panic setting in, knowing it was too soon for the baby to come, Amira called out for her husband.

***

Cries from his wife snatched Sheridan from his sleep. He rolled over, patting the bed. Realizing she wasn't there, he grabbed his robe, slid his feet into his slippers and followed the sound of her calling his name into the kitchen.

Focusing on a hunched over Amira, Sheridan almost stepped on a piece of glass.

"Watch out!" she warned as she leaned over the counter trying to again breathe her way through the pain.

Avoiding as much of the pool of hot water and glass as he could see, Sheridan rushed to the side of his obviously distraught wife.

"Amira baby, what's wrong."

She looked over at him, her eyes showing her pain. "I think I'm going into labor." Amira was panicking. "It's too soon Sheridan." She shook her head, fighting back tears.

As much as Amira had questioned whether or not she'd wanted this child early on, now that she'd been carrying it for 32 weeks she had come to love and accept this gift from God.

Sheridan scooped her into his arms, carrying her into the living room so that she didn't burn or cut herself. Placing her on the couch, he grabbed the phone from the cradle on the end table.

"How far apart are the contractions?" he asked as he pressed the speed dial number for her friend Carmen. They only lived two houses down and she was the closest to keep the kids while he took Amira to the hospital.

"I don't know! It's too soon Sheridan! It's too soon!"

He knelt in front of his wife, tightening his grip on her hand as he explained to Carmen the situation. He hung up the phone again, concentrating on the woman sitting in front of him.

"Calm down baby. How long ago was the last one?" He knew the doctor would want to know so he needed to find out how much time they had.

"I don't know Sheridan!"

He listened as she kept saying again and again that it was too soon. He needed her to calm down. Getting worked up would only intensify the contractions.

"Amira, listen to me. You're going to be fine." He covered her stomach with his hand, "Our baby's going to be fine as well. Now think. How long do you think it's been since you had the last contraction?"

As Amira thought about the question and finally gave him an answer, Sheridan made two more calls, one to the doctor and the other to Terrence. He'd call Tara on the way to the hospital, but Terrence was closer so he called him to relieve Carmen.

Turning his attention back to Amira, the ringing doorbell interrupted them.

"That's probably Carmen. Wait here. Let me let her in and then we'll go. Okay."

Amira nodded, her eyes following her husband as he dashed across the living room toward the front door. With Carmen two steps behind him he made his way back over to where his wife sat.

"Terrence should be here in a few minutes," Sheridan told Carmen as he helped Amira up from the couch. She squeezed his hand obviously having another contraction. Sheridan glanced at the clock on the wall. Thirteen minutes apart.

He grabbed his keys from the table by the door, helping Amira to the truck.

"Be careful in the kitchen. Amira dropped the coffee pot," Sheridan yelled back to Carmen as he rounded the truck.

"I'll take care of it," she replied as she waved good-bye to her friend.

With Amira secured in the passenger seat and one last glance at Carmen, Sheridan climbed into the truck and pulled out of the driveway headed for the hospital.

DOUBLETAKE

Sheridan

S heridan pulled the bedroom door closed, careful not to make a sound. Amira had finally gotten to sleep and the last thing he wanted to do was wake her. She'd been on bed rest for the last six weeks. The doctors had been able to stop her early labor and so far, she hadn't had any more contractions. She had a doctor appointment later in the day so she'd decided to get some rest.

Sheridan snickered to himself as he thought about how well Amira had adjusted to people doting on her hand and foot all hours of the day and night. He had promoted his most trusted foreman and delegated a significant amount of duties to the man so that he could be there for Amira when she needed him. They'd had quite a scare with the preterm labor and he wanted her life to remain as stress free as possible until this baby was born.

Making his way quietly down the hall, Sheridan entered the living room expecting to find Terrence and Tara in there watching television. Tara had taken the last three weeks off from work to help out around the house. She'd even moved into the guest house so if her sister needed her in the middle of the night, she'd be available.

Sheridan's hand hovered over the knob to the back door as he watched his best friend and sister-in-law sitting in front of the pond in his back yard. They did make a cute couple. Since the night he'd had to take Amira to the hospital, Sheridan had started to notice that the two seemed to be spending a lot more time together. Not to mention the looks he'd seen passed between them.

Sheridan stood in the doorway watching as Terrence slid a finger beneath Tara's chin. He raised her chin as he leaned down and kissed her. Sheridan only smiled to himself. He knew sooner or later those two would get together. Deciding to give them some privacy, he turned his attention to the television. He plopped down in the chair next to the empty playpen and began surfing channels. He hadn't realized how quiet the house was without the kids. Terrence had dropped Nasir off at school while he'd taken baby girl and his little man to daycare first thing this morning.

They'd decided it was best to have the kids away during the day. That way Amira wouldn't be worried about them if she went into labor again. Sheridan had even purchased a second set of car seats so that they didn't have to keep switching them back and forth between his and Terrence's vehicles.

Stopping on an episode of Overhaulin', Sheridan placed the remote on the end table and started watching the show.

"And how's the Mrs.?"

His attention caught up in the show, Sheridan hadn't noticed Terrence entering the house.

"She's asleep. I'm hoping the doctor will let her get out of that bed a little." Sheridan grabbed the remote, turning the volume down on the television just a little.

"Well it's almost over. When's she due?" Terrence claimed a seat on the couch, stretching his legs beneath the coffee table as he laid his head back.

"Two more weeks. But I don't think she's going to make it."

"Why you say that?" Terrence leaned up taking in the blank stare on his friend's face.

"Man, have you really looked at Amira lately. She's huge. The doctor said this is going to be a big baby."

"You two really ready for this?"

"I'm more than sure 'Mira is. I think since she had that scare, she's been keeping her fingers crossed to make it this far. At this point I just think she's ready to get this over with."

"And what about you?" Since Amira had gone into preterm labor, Terrence had watched the bond between his best friend and his wife reform. Sheridan hadn't mentioned the doubts he'd had earlier on in the pregnancy so Terrence was hoping that all of that was behind the happy couple.

"Yeah, I guess I'm ready. I mean, the nursery's done, the kids are excited about the new addition..." Sheridan kind of drifted off thinking about all of the changes they'd experience over the next few weeks.

"Sheridan!"

"Oh my bad." Sheridan shook the thoughts crowding

his mind. "Anyway what's up with you and Tara?"

"What you mean what's up with me and Tara?"

"Come on man." He eyed his boy waiting for him to respond.

"You know we just kickin' it."

"That kiss out there in the gardens didn't look like just kickin' it to me." Sheridan crossed his arms over his chest, glaring at his boy. He didn't want his sister-in-law getting hurt so if this was a game to Terrence, he wanted to stop this right now.

"Well you know," Terrence responded, not sure he really wanted to tell Sheridan everything that had been going on between him and Tara.

"Aye man. All I have to say is don't hurt her." Sheridan gave his friend a stern look. Tara wasn't just some chick he'd pick up in the club. She was family and although he and Terrence had been friends as far back as either of them could remember, family came first.

Terrence threw his hands up in surrender. "Naw man, it ain't even like that. Actually, I'm really feelin' Tara." Terrence glanced over his shoulder, watching from the living room as Tara cut roses off of the bush at the front of the guesthouse. He knew she'd sprinkle some of the pedals over her bed for them to enjoy later tonight.

"Feelin' her huh. Don't tell me the playa playa is thinking about the old ball and chain."

"Hey, I did tell you that I wanted to be just like you when I grew up. Maybe Tara has me thinking about growing up."

Terrence's gaze never wavered from that of his best friend as he said the words. For the most part, he agreed with Sheridan. Tara was family, not just to Amira and Sheridan, but to him as well. And the more time they spent together, the less time he wanted to spend without her.

"You? Grow up? If you say so. Just make sure you're ready."

Sheridan turned his attention back to the men dismantling a 1969 Dodge Mopar. He saw the sincerity in his best friend's face. He was falling for Tara. Assured that this was serious business, Sheridan chose to let grown folks handle their business. In the end, he was sure that Tara could tame that beast and maybe they'd all become one big happy family.

Two Tell the Truth...

DOUBLETAKE

Winston

Winston's eyes remained locked on the front door of Sheridan's house. He ignored the humming from the woman sitting in the car beside him. He'd just looked at the clock and if his calculations were correct, Sheridan would be leaving any minute now to drop the kids off before going to work.

He sunk into the seat, still trying to place the strange feeling he'd had over the last few months. He'd been craving the strangest foods and for some reason, he just couldn't shake the feeling that someone was pregnant. Jasmine had assured him it was all in his head. She was still on her birth control pills and they used condoms so she wasn't the one pregnant. They'd had a fight about it, ending with her accusing him of cheating. He'd almost slipped up and told her what he'd done but caught himself before the words fell from his mouth.

Winston slid his hands under his legs, warding off the uncontrollable tremble. He'd never been so nervous in his life. Well, maybe once, the first time he'd gotten caught stealing and hauled away to juvie. He'd beat the charge, something about the cop being intoxicated while making the arrest and he'd learned that day how to work the system. Still, he didn't have a reason to be shaking and yet he was doing just that.

"Winston? Winston!"

"What!" He responded to her beckon but continued to stare at his brother's house.

"Why are you shaking?"

He'd been so absorbed in his thoughts he hadn't taken the time to realize that Jasmine's hand was on his shoulder. "I don't know. A little nervous I guess."

"You can do this. All you have to do is talk to him."

Before he could think of a response, the front door a few houses down opened and Sheridan stepped out onto the porch. Winston's eyes widened to the size of golf balls when he laid eyes on Amira's obviously swollen belly. Any sound he thought of making dropped to the pit of his stomach. He forced his mouth to remain closed, keeping his teeth clenched. Winston closed his eyes, calculating the timing of his trip. Gauging the size of Amira's stomach, she was probably close to being due, putting the possibility of him being the father right at the top of the scale.

"Man, you two look just alike." Even from where they sat there was no denying that Winston and Sheridan were definitely brothers. There was no way for their parents to deny them.

Winston quickly regained his composure, hoping Jasmine hadn't noticed his change in demeanor. The last thing he wanted was for her to get suspicious. It was possible that he could be the child's father but until he had complete confirmation, he'd keep the suspicion to himself.

"I guess it's time for you to know the whole story. Sheridan and I aren't just brothers. We're twins." Since they'd started dating, Winston had kept that piece of information to himself. It wasn't important as far as he was concerned. He and Sheridan hadn't crossed paths since the day he'd left. The only reason Jasmine even knew he had a brother was because of his loudmouth mother.

"You mean you've had an identical twin out here all of these years and never told me. Why?" Jasmine didn't like the fact that Winston had kept this information from her. Having a brother was one thing but an identical one was another.

"First," Winston watched as Sheridan grabbed the youngest child from Amira's arms and kissed her good bye before carrying the little boy to the Tahoe parked in the driveway. "We're not identical."

"But you two look just alike. Are you sure?" She didn't care what he said; no two family members looked that much alike unless they were identical twins.

"Yes I'm sure. The doctors called us half-twins." Winston cut his eyes in her direction just to see if she was watching him or his brother.

"What?" She faced him, trying to understand what he meant by half-twin. She'd heard of fraternal and identical twins but half twins was a new one on her.

"Supposedly half-twin is how doctors can explain why some sets of twins look exactly alike but have slightly different DNA compositions. It happens when an egg splits before being fertilized and each half is fertilized by an individual sperm."

"Let me get this straight, one egg that splits, two sperm. So that would mean instead of sharing 100% DNA like identical twins or 50% like fraternal twins you two share, what, 75% of your DNA?"

"Very good," He gave her a proud look, a smile plastered across his face, "it usually takes people forever to figure that out. Since we look so much alike, we use to just tell people we're identical. It makes things so much easier. But our fingerprints are mirror images of each other. Also, I carry the sickle cell trait but Sheridan doesn't and my blood type is AB+ like our father, Sheridan's O- like mom."

Jasmine looked over at Winston, expecting him to be watching Sheridan pack the children into the vehicle. Instead his gaze stayed on the woman standing on the porch with her arms wrapped around her swollen belly.

"Why are you looking at her like that?" Jasmine allowed the rage to seep into her words. She wanted an answer and she wanted it now.

"No reason," he replied hoping the words hadn't come out too quickly, "I just didn't expect her to be pregnant again. They already have three kids. I knew my brother was fond of children but not that fond of them."

She studied him a moment more trying to determine if his answer satisfied her. She watched as he turned his attention to his brother. When his eyes stayed in that direction until he'd secured the last child in a car seat, she decided to drop it for now.

"He's leaving. What do you want to do?"

She kept her attention focused on her man. This was his

call. She'd promised to be there to support him but this was his family and it was his responsibility to try to mend things. If he didn't, she wasn't sure what kind of a future they'd have together. However, intervening would only make matters worse so she'd let him be the man and do this on his own.

"I'll come back later, try to catch up with him after he gets home from work."

Winston started up the rental vehicle, waiting until Sheridan passed them before turning around in one of the neighboring driveway. The sky above them started to cloud over, falling right in line with the way he felt right about now. He was glad Jasmine was letting him do this in his own time. He had plenty to think about. Mainly was he about to be a daddy?

Winston pulled to a stop in front of their hotel a little numb. The silence consuming the space in the vehicle had been welcomed for the twenty-minute drive from Sheridan's home to the place where he and Jasmine planned to spend the rest of the week.

She'd convinced him that a couple of days wouldn't be enough time for him and his brother to air out their differences and begin to move forward. He agreed, so they'd both taken a week and a half off from work to fly down and get this over with. Initially, Winston was glad she wanted to be there for him. Now though, if he truly believed what his heart was telling him, then he knew the end for them was all to near.

Winston climbed from the vehicle caught up in his own misery. He made his way to their room not even taking the time to notice that Jasmine stayed a few steps behind him, unusual for the woman who always believed a woman should walk at her man's side, not in his shadow. He waited for her before sliding the little plastic key through the electronic lock.

"I hope you don't think I'm ignoring you," he said to her.

Winston pulled her into his arms, needing to have her close. He'd spend his last few days with her making her feel like a queen. If Amira's baby was his, it wouldn't make up for what he'd done but he wanted Jasmine to know that he did love her no matter what.

"Winston, I don't know what to think. My woman's intuition is telling me that I'm missing something." She stared up into his brown eyes silently pleading for him to put her uneasiness to rest.

"It's nothing to worry your pretty little head over." He wrapped his arms around her, holding her in a warm loving embrace. He'd miss having her in his life but life on the streets had taught him to be realistic, nothing lasts forever.

He slid the card into the reader, backing them into the room. If she was going to be gone soon, he planned to please her in ways he'd never pleased her before. Allowing the hotel door to slam shut Winston wisped his woman away for possibly the last time.

Amira and Sheridan

Sheridan changed lanes, darting in and out of traffic trying to get to his wife as quickly as possible. He grabbed his cell phone, dialing Terrence's number. "Come on, come on. Answer."

"Aye," Sheridan cut in front of another SUV slipping between a Mazda and an old Cadillac. He was glad Terrance was answering his phone. Usually when he was in a meeting he, let calls go to voicemail. "I need you to get the kids. Amira just went into labor." He flipped on the turn signal again changing lanes to get around a motorist driving slower than he wanted to go. "I'll call you when I know something."

He hung up the phone, continuing his race toward the hospital. He picked up the ringing cell phone, glancing at the caller id before taking the call. Realizing it was Tara he flipped the phone open.

"How is she?" Sheridan floored the gas, passing an eighteen-wheeler and cutting into the left lane.

Tara informed him that Amira was progressing fast. The nurses said she'd probably be ready to push in another hour or so. That still gave him plenty of time to get to the hospital and to be there for the delivery. She needed him and if it was the last thing he did, he'd be there.

"Tell her I'm on my way. I should be there in another fifteen minutes. And make sure you tell her that I love her."

Tara assured him that she would deliver the message and that she'd call him back if anything changed.

Hanging up the phone, Sheridan continued to bob and weave through traffic, praying to not get a ticket. He honked his horn, swerving in front of a motorist driving 45mph in the far left lane. He hoped his driving like a mad man wouldn't draw too much attention and get him pulled over.   Ten more minutes of driving like a madman and praying like there was no tomorrow, Sheridan lucked up on a parking spot on the third level of the deck adjacent to the hospital. As he dashed across the covered walkway, he answered his ringing cell phone knowing instinctively that it was Tara.

"What room?" he asked, dancing from one foot to the other while the glowing numbers of the elevator lit one by one in a descending order. She gave him the room number, instructing him to hurry if he wanted to see his child born.

Sheridan jumped on the elevator inside of the hospital, relieved that he was the only person on it. The button numbered three lit to a soft red as he punched it three or four times. He knew it wouldn't make a difference how many times he pressed the button, the elevator wasn't going to move any faster and yet his finger continued to jab the little plastic button.

Stepping from the elevator, he caught a nurse by the arm nearly scaring the woman half to death. "Can you tell me where room 312 is?"

She pointed to the right and Sheridan took off in that direction, dodging a man exiting one room and a woman who was entering another. He swung the door open, taking in the sight of his wife's legs being held up by Tara and the nurse.

The bed sheets were bunched in Amira's fingers as she concentrated on pushing. Immediately, Sheridan was by her side. She looked over at him and smiled as she took a short rest waiting for the next contraction.

Tears streamed down her cheeks as the next wave of pain and the urge to push again overwhelmed her. Her nails digging into his palm, Sheridan focused on encouraging his wife. He was more than sure things had progressed so fast that she hadn't gotten any medication and if she was okay enduring the pain, then the least he could do was bear it with her.

"All right Mrs. Malcolm. One more push should do it."

Sheridan wiped the sweat and tears from his wife's face as she concentrated on breathing. "Almost there baby."

She took in one last deep breath, leaning up and bearing down. Sheridan leaned over, watching as a head full of curly black hair peeped from his wife's body followed by a not so happy looking face, shoulders, chest, stomach, legs and feet. He smiled as the doctor placed the squirming wiggling baby on Amira's stomach.

"Mr. Malcolm, would you like to do the honors?"

As he'd done with their three previous children, Sheridan grabbed the scissors from the doctor and cut his son's cord. The nurse quickly wrapped the little bundle of joy up in a blanket moving him to a warmer while they drew blood and check him out. The baby was good sized, a relief for both mother and father considering he was almost two weeks early.

Sheridan had dropped everything at the call from Amira informing him that her water had broken. He'd initially panicked thinking that she was at home alone. She'd calmed him down, telling him that Tara was there and they were on their way out of the door. He was more than glad they'd decided to take both of the little ones to daycare until the baby was born.

Sheridan turned his attention from the nurses tending to his son to his wife. This pregnancy had been so much harder on her than the other three and not just because he'd been around less. Since the preterm labor scare, things had been hard. She'd developed gestational diabetes in her last trimester causing her to have to completely adjust her eating habits. Checking her blood sugar every few hours had initially been a pain but she'd gotten used to it.

Then, she'd slipped almost into a state of depression a couple of weeks earlier when she'd started spotting. Though the doctor had allowed her to go home, she was put on strict bed rest in hopes of keeping the baby from delivering for at least another week. She'd made it to thirty-eight weeks, but she was still two before her due date. All of that was behind them now. From what they could tell, they had another perfect addition to their family.

"Would you like to hold your son?"

Sheridan looked over at the nurse holding his little boy out to him. He cradled his little bundle of joy, holding him close to his heart. His heart warmed as his son locked eyes with him just as he'd done with his mother the few moments after he'd made his grand entrance into this world.

A few minutes of bonding with his son and Sheridan relinquished the little boy to his wife, hoping that little Tariq Jamal Malcolm would take to nursing immediately as his greedy older brothers and sister had. When the little boy latched on, suckling from Amira's breast Sheridan whispered in his wife's ear, "I'll love you and him for all eternity."

She understood the promise. It was the same promise he'd given to her immediately after each of their children was born. It was his reassurance to her that no matter what, he'd be by her side.

The new little family cuddled together, bonding. All of the previous worrying, all of the sadness about having a new addition to their ever growing family, all doubts disappeared as Amira and Sheridan held on to each other and their son. They'd believed things would work themselves out and with the birth of this precious little boy, they had.

DOUBLETAKE

Sheridan

Sheridan rocked in the hospital chair with his son cradled in his arms just enjoying the feel of this little life that he'd been a part of creating. He stared at Amira as she lay in her hospital bed taking a nap. They'd had a steady stream of visitors and deliveries since early in the morning. But things had slowed down. Carmen and Madison had stepped out for a little while to give the new parents some time alone to bond with their new little one. Tara assured them that she and Terrance could handle the other kids so Sheridan had stayed the night in the hospital to help Amira as much as possible. He figured one or both of them should be on the way to the hospital now to visit.

Sheridan had seen the exhaustion in his wife, and especially so after the first hours after delivery. He'd never seen her this tired. Her delivery was fairly short, only a couple of hours but this pregnancy had worn her down in ways he'd never seen his wife worn down. The doctor had warned them that her progression might be quicker this time, considering the time between the first stages of labor and delivery had decreased with each of their children. The man seemed almost surprised that Amira had had the couple of hours that she'd had.

Placing his now sleeping son on his wife's stomach Sheridan reached for the envelope on the tray table next to the bed. They'd request a copy of the baby's medical test to add to their files. He and Terrence had a bet running to see what this baby's blood type was going to be. Sheridan had missed the doctor's morning visit when he'd gone to get something to eat while Amira fed their little one.

Curious to see if Tariq had kept with the pattern of having his daddy's blood type, Sheridan slid the paperwork from the envelope. The boys were both A and baby girl was B. Since he was O and Amira was AB he expected his son to be either A or B. To his surprise though the blood type listed for Tariq was AB+. Confused, Sheridan continued to read, discovering that Tariq also carried the sickle cell trait. Grabbing the notebook with his and Amira's medical history, he went back through each set of previous blood test. Each one indicted that neither he nor Amira carried the sickle cell trait. So how was it that Tariq carried it?

Sheridan left his sleeping wife and son to find the doctor. Hopefully she could shed some light on the situation. He lucked up as the pudgy woman in the white coat stepped from another room. She stopped in the hallway, looking down at the chart in her hand. He hadn't meant to startle her, but he needed answers to the questions dancing in his mind.

"Can I ask you a question?" He still held the paper and apparently she'd seen the document because her demeanor changed the moment her eyes left his hand.

"What can I do for you Mr. Malcolm?" She plastered a non-convincing smile on her face.

"Well, I was wondering, is it possible for a child to carry the sickle cell trait without one of the parents carrying it?" He needed her to say yes. If she didn't say yes, Sheridan didn't know what he was going to do.

The woman looked up at the concern on the face of the man towering over her. Based on his reaction, she suspected he was just starting to put the pieces together. She wondered if he'd figured out the blood type issue as well. It wasn't her place to say anything so she'd had a brief conversation with Amira earlier telling her that she needed to look over her child's medical information very carefully.

"As far as I know, the answer to your question is no." The woman reached down, reading the text message on her ringing pager, "I really need to get going. You should talk to your wife, Mr. Malcolm." She turned, walking down to the next room and entering before he had the chance to stop her.

Sheridan stood there in the middle of the hallway completely numb. This couldn't be happening. Tariq looked just like him. This wasn't happening. She didn't cheat. This had to be a mistake. His feet dragged as he walked past room after room of happy couples waiting for or just receiving a special delivery. With each step down the hallway, the disbelief changed to anger. The hall seemed longer, like the closer he got the further away the door to his wife's room appeared. By the time he reached the door, all he felt was fury. He flung the door open, not caring whether he woke Amira or the baby. He wanted answers and he wanted them now and nothing short of a miracle was going to stop him from getting them.

Sheridan ignored the screaming child, placing the baby not so gently into the bassinet by the bed. "What the fuck is this!" He nearly shoved the papers down Amira's throat.

Pussyfooting around this wasn't going to happen. This was a straight answer question.

"Why are you yelling? You're scaring the baby." She reached over, planning to calm Tariq but Sheridan stepped between them.

"I don't give a damn! You got some fuckin' explaining to do. That baby," he pointed at the hollering infant, "Ain't mine!" He glared at her, his mind still having a hard time understanding why she'd cheated and how long had it been going on.

He just couldn't comprehend it; he always did for her. Whatever she needed, he made sure she got. He worked his ass off so that she didn't have to work. He sacrificed so much of his time making sure she didn't want for anything and this is how she repaid him. Well never again. No more; he was done. This was something he could never forgive her for; never.

"What are you talking about? Of course Tariq is yours." Amira stared at her husband, her face questioning why he'd think that Tariq wasn't his. How could he accuse her of such a thing, especially after he'd been MIA for most of her pregnancy? If anything, she should be questioning his fidelity.

"I can't believe you're sitting here fucking lying to me!" He threw the papers in her face so that she could get a good look at them. Maybe she hadn't seen the information or maybe she was just trying to play him like she'd had to do to make him believe that baby was his.

Now that he thought about it, maybe that's why he'd never had cravings like he had with the other kids. Maybe this baby wasn't two weeks early. Maybe she was already pregnant the night he'd come back from his business trip. That would mean that the baby was only a few days early. Things were starting to make sense now he just wished he'd have figured it out sooner.

Sheridan watched as Amira's eyes widened at the information on the paper. "I- I don't know what to say. There has to be some sort of mistake. We have to talk to the doctor. Maybe there was some mix up with the blood tests."

"I already talked to the doctor; ain't no fucking mistake! You're ass fucked up and now you fuckin' caught." He walked back and forth in the narrow space between his wife and the obviously distraught baby. He couldn't even bring himself to look at the boy. He'd been such a fool.

"Look at that baby, Sheridan! He looks just like you, just like all the other kids. I didn't do anything Sheridan; you have to believe me." Amira pleaded with her husband to think rationally about this but his expression told her that he was far beyond rational right now. "I didn't do anything. There has to be some mistake! I didn't do anything."

Amira tried to fight back the tears but between Sheridan's pacing and accusations, her newborn baby crying his poor little heart out and all of her hormones still way out of whack, she couldn't fight it. She grasped her chest, starting to hyperventilate. She expected her husband to at least try to get her calmed down but all he did was glare at her like she was a piece of trash on the street. She couldn't breath, she couldn't respond. She didn't know what was happening and right now she didn't know that she cared to.

Sheridan stepped closer, hovering only inches away from Amira's face, "You know what, you a low down, dirty, trifling ho. I guess my son did see somebody creeping out of our bedroom that night."

"Mr. Malcolm! I think it's time for you to leave."

Sheridan turned around at the sound of a female voice. He narrowed his eyes at the woman he'd spoken to earlier. His eyes then locked with the hospital security guard standing next to the doctor. He cut his eyes back at Amira, whispering a few inches from her face, "Don't worry, I'll make sure my real kids are taken care of."

He backed off, glancing one last time at the crying infant to his left before he walked past the security guard and the doctor and out of the door. He didn't have anything else to say to her anyway. As far as he was concerned, his marriage was more than over.

Winston

Winston rolled to a stop a few houses down from Sheridan's most impressive home. He turned his eyes towards the sky, watching as it darkened. He smelled rain, the gloom of the day matching his mood to the letter. He put the vehicle in park, taking a minute to gather his thoughts and his nerves. He'd tried to figure out what he was going to say to his brother, had spent most of the night up worrying about it, but he still hadn't figured it out. He'd considered just going back home, but Jasmine's constant urging and encouragement finally gave him incite enough to realize that until he faced his past, his future would continue to have a grim cloud hovering over it.

He reached for the door, prepared to exit when he noticed movement from the house. Winston stopped, watching as his brother dragged suitcases and a number of boxes out of the front door. Winston sat there a few minutes more as his brother carried more bags and boxes from the home. He'd even taken the car seats out to make more room. What was he doing?

Needing to talk to him before he left, Winston climbed out of the rental and headed down past the manicured lawns and brick and stone mailboxes. Closing the distance between him and his brother, his pace slowed. He never took his eyes off of the face so much like his own. He ignored the light drizzle beginning or at least as much as he could. By the look of things, the bottom could fall out of the sky at any moment.

Walking down the sidewalk, coming ever closer to his destiny, Winston listened to his brother rant and rave about the baby. And he didn't like what he heard. He stopped at the line of bushes at the end of the driveway. Standing to the side just enough so that he had a good view of Sheridan but the trees kept him hidden, Winston listened.

Fuck that! There's no way that baby could be mine!

Winston watched as Sheridan lifted one of the suitcases and slid it into the back seat of the truck. His brother reached down, grabbing one of the boxes and placing it into the truck as well.

I know but neither of us carries the sickle cell trait. The only way that baby could have gotten it was if his real daddy gave it to him.

No. No. No. Winston began feeling light headed. The longer he listened to his brother's conversation, the more of a bad feeling crept into his heart. He'd thought that Amira looked like she was ready to drop that baby any day now but he'd hope to have the chance to talk to Sheridan before she did.

I don't give a damn if he looks just like me. That ain't my baby!

Sheridan slammed the truck's door, leaning his back against it. Winston watched as his brother pulled out a pocketknife and cut the little plastic wristband from his arm. The band sailed in the wind for a minute before coming to rest on the ground. His brother stomped on it before heading back into the house.

Guessing Sheridan was about to leave, Winston made a mad dash back to his vehicle. Now he'd really done it. He needed to find out if his sister-in-law's baby was his. But first, he needed to find out where his brother was going. Sliding down in the seat, making sure Sheridan didn't see him, Winston waited for his brother's vehicle to pass. From the glimpse through the window, he was pretty sure that his brother was still on the phone. Allowing him to put a little distance between them, Winston started his vehicle and circled around.

They drove down the road for twenty minutes, though with all of the turns, it felt like hours. Winston stayed a few car lengths behind just to make sure Sheridan didn't suspect he was being followed. The man turned into an upscale town home community and Winston followed suit. It was going to be a little harder to stay hidden now but he rolled at a very slow place so that if Sheridan looked back, he'd think the person in the vehicle behind him was looking for someone's address.

When Sheridan parked next to a fire engine red Mercedes Benz, Winston pulled into a parking space two buildings down. He sat in his vehicle observing his brother grabbing a bag and a box from the truck and carrying it up to the door. He waited as Sheridan and his boy unloaded the remainder of the items packed in the truck. With the last box in hand, the two men entered the town home and closed the front door.

Winston tried to stay calm. He replayed the events of the last half an hour over and over in his mind. Sheridan had said that the baby looked just like him, something Winston had expected of course, but the sickle cell trait was the key piece of information that made him know in his heart that Amira's baby was his child.   Their mother had always cautioned him that if he ever got serious with a woman and decided he wanted to have a family, he needed to verify that she didn't carry the sickle cell trait. That one piece of information could determine if his child just carried the trait or could possibly end up with sickle cell disease.

Damn. Winston just sat there in disbelief. He had a child now and he wanted to do the right thing but he had no clue how to go about doing that. He took in a deep breath his mind formulating a plan. He needed to see his child and he needed to get a DNA test just to make sure. Pulling out of the parking spot, Winston started calling hospitals. He'd find where his child was, he'd get a DNA test and then he'd try to figure out what to do next.

***

Standing at the window of the hospital nursery Winston stared at the quiet child lying in the bassinet labeled Malcolm. He'd considered posing as his twin to get a closer look at the child but he wanted to wait. He'd found a young lady who'd been willing to do a DNA test for a little cold hard cash. One thing about the good old US of A, money talked. Two grand cash was a drop in the bucket if that baby was his.

Sheridan was right about one thing though, that baby did look just like them. Winston was surprised that his brother didn't even suspect that maybe he'd had something to do with this. True enough they hadn't been a part of each other's lives in a long time, but he was sure that if he was in his brother's shoes, knowing what he knew, he'd suspect his twin might have had a hand in this. Then again, Sheridan always wanted to believe the best in people. Even when they'd switched girlfriends, he'd always believed that Winston never crossed the line. As long as he never found out otherwise, Sheridan was happy accepting that people stuck to their word. Sheridan was the straight and narrow guy and he the risk taker. Now that risk taking had caught up to him and any chance of reconciling with his brother lay in the hands of a DNA test.

Winston glanced over his shoulder at the sound of a woman clearing her throat. He hadn't expected her back for at least another couple of hours, giving him more time to convince himself that this really wasn't happening.

"Done so soon?"

"Let's just say I took care of this one personally. Did you get what you needed for your part of the bargain?" She stepped up next to him, using the wall as a barrier between her and the nurses tending to the infants in the nursery.

Winston slid a bulky white envelope from the inside pocket of his jacket. "You don't need to count it. It's all there." He handed the envelope to the short honey brown woman with the seventies styled glasses. Though he continued to watch the sleeping child caught in the middle of this mess, he took glimpses of her out the corner of his eye. He thought she was kinda cute. She'd look better with her hair up out of her face but the style didn't make her any less attractive. Under any other circumstances, he'd have gotten her number but flirting was the last thing on his mind.

"Nice doing business with you." She grabbed the envelope, handed him the brown one she held in her hands and darted off around the corner.

Winston stared at the package in his hand and then backed up at the baby dressed in powder blue with a royal blue hat on his head. Royal blue. Sheridan's favorite color. He didn't need this test to tell him that was his son. Something inside already knew.   Winston flipped the envelope over, sliding his finger beneath the flap. He pulled the white piece of paper half way out, staring only at the number on the page; 99.998%. That number meant everything he'd ever known, everything he'd ever worked for had just changed. He was on the verge of gaining so much and now he was more than sure he was about to lose it all.

Winston didn't know what to feel. He wanted to hold his son. He wanted to tell the world that he was a proud father and that he'd be there forever breathe, every step, every cry of that little boy's life. And yet, he had no way of knowing how any of that was going to happen. Happy in ways, saddened in others, and more confused than he'd ever been in his life, Winston turned his back to the life he'd help create and walked away.

Winston

Winston stood outside the door of the suite he shared with Jasmine, a bottle of scotch in one hand and the key card in the other. He'd driven around long enough to run out a full tank of gas and he'd sat outside of the place where his brother had moved for another few hours, trying to get up the nerve to ring the bell. Finally, giving up on doing this tonight, he'd filled the tank on the rental and made a run for the liquor store. He'd already decided that he'd tell Jasmine about the baby tonight. There was no reason to lead her on in this. His priority was his son and if she wasn't going to be by his side in this, then it was best she walk away now.

He stared at the lock, contemplating. He listened for any sound coming from the other side of the door. No light escaped from beneath it so he assumed she was either out or asleep. He hated to wake her. Maybe he'd tell her in the morning, might even get him a little before she walked out of his life.

Twirling the card between his fingers one last time, Winston's hand crept closer to the electronic pad. With one quick dip of the plastic card, the little light turned from red to green and he heard the lock click. His fingers wrapped around the ice-cold handle and he turned it. Pushing the door open, he slipped into the room somewhat comforted by the darkness. He pushed the door up slowly, hoping to not wake Jasmine if she was already asleep.

With the door secured, Winston walked past the bathroom expecting to find Jasmine curled up under the covers in the king sized bed. Instead, she stood out on the balcony, dressed in a sheer nightgown, staring up at the sky. Plopping down on the bed, he put the bottle of scotch on the nightstand before pouring himself a drink. He turned the glass up, not letting the liquid touch his tongue as the liquid burned a trail down to his stomach.

"Winston."

He couldn't look up at her, not knowing what he had to tell her. She meant so much to him. He'd never loved another woman the way he loved Jasmine; well, maybe one, but that was a long time ago.

"Winston, where have you been?"

She sounded close. She must have come in from the balcony. He flinched as her hand came to rest on his shoulder.

"I've been worried about you Winston. I've been calling you all day. You didn't answer your phone or pager. Where you been, baby?"

"Handling business." The words came out dry, just like his throat. He reached over, filling the glass with ice and pouring himself another shot.

Jasmine sat on the bed next to him. She wrapped an arm around his shoulder attempting to comfort him.

He shrugged her off. Grabbing his drink, he made his way out onto the balcony. Leaning over onto the banister Winston watched the city lights wishing things were different. She didn't deserve this. She didn't deserve to have her heart broken. But before tonight was over, he'd do just that.

"What happened Winston?"

This time she kept her distance. He felt her eyes boring into his soul. She knew something was up; he could feel it. Sooner or later he was going to have to tell her. Better sooner than later.

Now or never he answered her plea. "I fucked up baby. I fucked up so bad this time I don't think there is any way out of this one."

"It can't be that bad. Did you talk to Sheridan?"

"Not yet." He took another swig from his drink, wishing he'd brought the rest of the bottle with him. As if she'd read his mind, she topped off his glass. Reading his desire for more personal space, she placed the bottle on the patio table and took a seat in one of the chairs.

"If you didn't talk to Sheridan, then what's the problem?"

"The problem is, you're about to walk out of my life." He looked up at the sky, squeezing his eyes shut, fighting back an aching from a place inside that he'd never felt anything, that place where he assumed a deep caring for one's soul mate resided.

"What are you talking about? I'm not going anywhere." The pitch in her voice rose. He heard the fear in it and the confusion.

"Yes you are. You just don't know it yet." His head dropped his arm reaching up to massage the back of his neck.

"Winston, you're starting to scare me. Tell me what's going on."

Taking in a deep breath, Winston started, "I found out something today. Something I did has probably ruined somebody's life."

Jasmine remained quiet; trying her best to figure out what it was he'd done that was so bad that he felt it had ruined someone's life.

"Whose life Winston?" She finally asked.

Winston looked over at her. Her eyes were turned down, focused on her hands just sitting in her lap. He expected hand ringing, sadness, some sign of emotion. Instead from what he could see, she kept a blank expression.

He went to her, kneeling beside the woman he wanted to spend the rest of his life with. He'd be a man about this though. She deserved that much.

"Sheridan's wife had the baby yesterday…" His voice trailed off as she turned worried eyes up at him.

"That's a good thing right? The baby's okay, isn't it?"

He observed the worry. Not knowing was getting to her. "Yes. The baby is completely healthy. But I went to see Sheridan. I'd planned on trying to talk to him but when I got to the house, he was packing his bags."

"He was moving out?" That didn't make sense. If his

wife had just had a baby, why would he be moving out?

"The baby's not his." He lowered his eyes, ashamed of what he'd done and what he was about to do. But the past was the past and only by telling the truth on this one would he have even an ounce of peace in his heart.

"Oh Winston I'm sorry…" She kept her hands to herself, sensing that he didn't want to be babied.

"Wait. Before you go feeling sorry for my family, there's more." He covered her hands with his, wanting to touch her a few moments more before she walked away for good. This was it, the instant before she left him for all eternity. "I overheard him on the phone at the house. He said that the baby looked just like him but he carries the sickle cell trait."

Jasmine narrowed her eyes at the man sitting across from her. She pulled her hands away and slid further from him. She shook her head while saying the words. "What are you saying, Winston?"

Here it was, the moment of truth. "When I came down the first time, Sheridan was out of town." He stood, giving her the space she obviously wanted. No reason to pretend anymore. This was already over. "When I saw how picture perfect his life was, all I wanted to do was make him pay for what he'd done to me. That could have been my life. That was supposed to be me."

He stopped, waiting for her to say something, anything but she didn't. He turned his back to her, not able to look her in the face. He wanted to, but just like he'd always done before, he ran when things got too hot.

"So, I decided to get even. I spent a little time out with some other women, making sure his wife's friends saw me.

Apparently he never told her that he had a brother, so they assumed I was him. But Sheridan's wife wasn't buying it so I stepped things up a notch. I'd planned to just leave some things in the house, get her to thinking that he might be doing something while he was out of town. I snuck into their bedroom and she was just laying there naked…"

"Please Winston. Please tell me you didn't do what I think you did."

The tears in her eyes pour out through her voice. He heard the trembling, the underlying fear that all she'd invested in him all of these years could be snatched away just that easily. He didn't mean for this to happen, but he couldn't go back and change it.

Winston poured his guts out to her. He told her everything, how he slept with Amira and how the minute he realized what he'd done, he regretted it. She didn't need to hear the gory details but he made sure she understood. When he turned around to face her, she just stared at him in disbelief. She'd trusted him, even encouraged him to try to work things out with his brother. Instead, he'd made things that much worse and not just for himself.

Jasmine stood. On the verge of storming out, she glared at him. If looks could kill, he'd be buried six feet under by now.

"You nasty, selfish bastard. You're right; you did fuck up this time. All this time," she allowed the tears to fall, the hurt running rampant through her body. She loved him so much. She hated to leave him, but it was something she had to do. He'd left her with no other options. "All this time you knew what you'd done. How could you? How could you come back into our bed after what you did? How could you ruin that woman's life like this!" She wrapped her arms around her body, backing away as he tried to close the distance between them. "You know I don't get you. First you say you want to work things out, that you miss having your brother in you life. Then you turn around and do this."

Winston reached out to her, for her.

"Don't touch me! Don't you ever touch me again!" She turned, somehow managing to make her way into the room she'd shared with him since they'd arrived in Atlanta. Grabbing her suitcase, jacket, and her purse, she stormed to the door. She opened it, not turning to face him when she said the last words she'd ever speak to him. "By the time you get home, I'll be gone." With that said, she walked out of the door.

Jasmine didn't know what she'd do about her job but right now she had to get away from him. He'd just broken the few things she still had control over, her spirit and her heart.

No woman, a son he may not ever get to see, his brother hating him for the rest of his life. Winston's life was getting more pitiful by the minute. He poured another glass of scotch, drinking the liquid in one gulp. His fingers tightened around the glass, squeezing as the hurt turned to something he'd only known once before. He hurled the glass at the side of the building and as it shattered against the gray stucco, his heart broke into just as many pieces.

DOUBLETAKE

Sheridan

Terrance descended the stairs headed towards the door to answer the ringing of the bell. He'd thought Sheridan was going to get it, considering he was downstairs in the living room but apparently he still wasn't in the mood to talk to anyone. Taking in the sight through the peephole, Terrence's mouth turned down in a frown. He opened the door staring at the man that he knew about but had never formally met.

Immediately, the pieces fell into place, the baby looking just like Sheridan but not matching in blood type, the sickle cell trait. Terrance glared at Winston, not believing the man had the audacity to be standing on his doorstep. And how'd he find out where Sheridan was? Not even Tara knew he'd come over here.

"Look, I don't want no trouble; I just really need to talk to my brother." Winston looked up at the man standing between him and his twin. He told himself again that he had to do this, that somehow he had to make things right; if not for himself, for Amira and his son.

Terrence signaled for Winston to step back, giving him room to step outside. He pulled the door up just enough to keep Sheridan, from hearing them. "What makes you think he'd even want to talk to you after what you did?"

"So he knows?" Winston winced. If anyone should have told Sheridan it should have been him.

"No. Fortunately for you, Sheridan is trusting. He hasn't figure out what you did. I however have. You know, that's some lowdown shit, even for you."

"This is between me and my brother…" This man had no right to be all up in his face telling him anything. He wasn't family. Hell, Winston didn't even know who this guy was.

"Wrong; this use to be between just you and your brother until you dragged Amira and my Godchildren into it. Now, it's my business too."

"Look. I came here to try to somehow fix this. I just want to do what's right for Tariq. I may have lost my chance at having my brother back in my life but I can still make sure that my son has a good home."

"Whoa, let me stop you right there. What makes you think you have any say so in what happens to that baby? You were an unwanted sperm donor and that's all." Terrence crossed his arms, his face turning up into a scowl. There was no way in hell this punk was being a father to that baby. Even if Sheridan walked out on Amira, Terrance would step in for the kids if the need arose. Though after realizing that Amira probably hadn't known it was his twin she'd slept with, Terrence was more than sure Sheridan would rethink walking out on his family.

"We'll see what my brother has to say about that. Now, do you mind?" As far as Winston was concerned, this discussion was over. No matter what this guy thought, family business stayed family business.

"Not at all." Fed up with this as well, Terrence opened the door. Stepping inside he called, "Sheridan, you got a visitor!"

"I don't want to see anyone right now." As if he didn't have enough to deal with. The last thing he wanted to do was talk to anybody.

"Oh I think you might want to see this one. It's your brother."

Terrance stepped to the side allowing, Winston to enter his home. As far as he knew, he was the only person Sheridan had told that he and his brother were twins. Sheridan kept a few things at Terrance's house and among those were any pictures he may have had of him and his brother together. He only held on to a few of them but lately, when he'd come to hang out, he'd spent time flipping through the albums.

Sheridan jumped up from the couch at the mention of his brother. Could this day get any worse? He'd spent most of the morning trying to put the pieces together. None of this made any sense. It bothered him that the baby looked so much like him and yet he didn't have a plausible blood type. Then, with the fact that his brother had been on his mind so much lately, Winston's obvious attempts to avoid his phone calls and now, him being here, Sheridan wondered.

Terrance climbed the stairs, leaving the two men to catch up. He hoped that they'd be civil. Of course, he knew otherwise and had more than prepared himself for whatever damage might be done to his home as a result of any altercation between them.

"What do you want Winston; this isn't exactly a good time." Sheridan crossed his arms over his chest, glaring at his brother. Seventeen years had passed and not a word. What was the point of him showing up now?

Winston closed the distance between them but tried his best to stay at least an arm's length away. He accepted this was the end of any possibility of reconciliation between them. Still he wanted to be a part of his son's life and, in order to do that, he had to tell Sheridan the truth. If his brother walked out on his family because of what he'd done, Winston would never forgive himself.

"I really think you need to go back home to your family." Winston leaned against the crown molding of the entryway to a fairly large room with a couch, matching chairs and a china cabinet.

"My family doesn't concern you. This is none of your business. And how'd you find me anyway?" The longer he stared at his brother, the greater the bad feeling creeping through his body.

"That's not important." Short, simple, to the point. Maybe this was a case of the less he said, the better.

"Spill it, Winston. You wouldn't have tracked me down if you didn't have something to say so go ahead and say it so you can go back to doing whatever it is you've been doing for the last seventeen years."

Sheridan didn't have the time or the patience to be dealing with this right now. All he wanted was to be by himself. He could tolerate Terrence but dealing with Winston right now was out of the question. Watching his twin closely, Sheridan realized that Winston appeared edgy. His left ear twitched and he'd never seen his brother's hands shake so much. If he didn't know any better, he'd have sworn Winston was nervous.

As the little metaphorical light bulb over his head burst to life, Sheridan narrowed his eyes at his brother. "What did you come here for?"

Winston had prepared this long drawn out explanation but at this moment, he couldn't bring himself to say the words. He pulled a folded piece of paper from his jacket pocket and handed it to his brother. The words on the page said all he had to say. There wasn't enough apologizing in the world to fix this so he wasn't even going to pretend like it would make a difference.

Sheridan felt the little vein on the side of his head begin to pulse as he read the words and the numbers on the page. The place in his mind where reason resided shut down as his blood boiled. He ground his teeth, closing his eyes, trying his best to calm down.

"I take full responsibility for everything. Amira didn't know. Between the pills and the alcohol, I'm more than sure she didn't even realize what happened."

How dare he? After all of this time, how dare he? Sheridan remembered the words he'd said to his wife in the hospital. He'd called his wife out of her name, said so many horrible things to her, accused her of infidelity and his own brother had been the truly guilty party. There wasn't a word in the English language that Sheridan could use to describe his feelings. Anger, fury, rage; none of them was strong enough to truly express what he felt.

It actually took Sheridan a few moments to comprehend what his brother had just said. He'd just confirmed that this really wasn't Amira's fault. She'd been completely out of it when this nasty bastard had come into their bedroom and defiled her body. Sheridan rushed his brother and before he knew it he'd punched Winston in the face. Stunned, Winston didn't move fast enough to miss getting caught in his brother's grasp. The next thing he knew, the coffee table gave way to his weight being flung across the room. He slid, hitting his head on the edge of the china cabinet, opening up a gash that started spurting blood. Luckily, the glass doors were locked so the dishes, now collapsing along with the shelves, didn't splatter all over the floor.

Getting to his feet, Winston dodged another flying fist only to trip over the couch, sending him barreling into one of the chairs. With a sharp pain in his back, Winston saw the wall progressing at him at an alarming rate and before he could get his hands up to brace the impact, he plowed into the wall. Falling to his knees, he tried to swing on Sheridan but his brother jerked back, missing the brow by only inches.

Within seconds, Sheridan was on his brother pounding him like a boxer plundering a weakened opponent. Winston tried to stop him, blocking the punches, pushing him away, but his brother just kept pounding his face with his fist. Gaining a little strength, Winston rolled, sending Sheridan to the floor. Winston tried to get up but Sheridan grabbed him by the ankle, sending him face first into the floor. With one hand, Sheridan flipped his brother over, wrapping his hands around his throat and cutting off his airway. Not thinking clearly, he continued to squeeze as his brother squirmed beneath him, clawed at his wrist, gasped for air.

"Sheridan, stop! You're going to kill him!" Terrence

rushed into the room, realizing that the fight had gotten way out of hand. He raced to the other side of the room putting Sheridan in a head lock and pulling back, hoping to turn his attention away from what he was doing long enough to get him to come to his senses.

"Sheridan, think about what you're doing. What he did was wrong, but Amira and the kids need you here with them, not in jail."

With the words sinking into his mind, Sheridan's grip on Winston's neck loosened. Terrence pulled him away, turning him around and making sure he stayed between the two men. Sheridan looked up as his brother rolled over into a kneeling position on the floor, trying to catch his breath. Taking in the bloody nose and swollen lip of his twin Sheridan walked out of the room headed for the kitchen. The next thing they knew, the back door slammed shut, shaking the walls of the townhouse.

Terrence eyed Winston. "The bathroom's down the hall. Try not to bleed on my floors." He left the beaten and stunned man lying on the floor trying to compose himself. Winston was the least of his concerns. He needed to make sure that Sheridan didn't do anything he'd regret.

DOUBLETAKE

Sheridan

errance watched his best friend walk the narrow path between the back door and the patio furniture. He waited for Sheridan to make the first move. He couldn't even fathom what that man was going through.

Sheridan stopped only a step away from the glass bar. He walked behind the chest high table, reaching for the door of the hidden refrigerator.

"It's empty," Terrance said, knowing what Sheridan was looking for.

"I need a drink." He continued to ramble behind the bar hoping his friend was just kidding. There had to be something back here that would numb the anger and the hurt. He'd been a fool and now he had to go home and face his wife. Sheridan had not only just lost all respect for his twin brother but from this day forward, some part of him would always question any man's intentions when it came to his wife; even Terrance's. Sheridan didn't know what sort of strain this might put on his friendship but if family would do this to him, he didn't know what to expect from his friends or his enemies.

"Alcohol is the last thing you need right now," Terrence said to the still angry man. "Drinking will only make you more irrational. You needed to keep a clear head. Someone has to break the news to Amira and right now you're the one person at the top of the list."

"Don't tell me what the fuck I need!" He slammed the fridge door closed, running his hand over his freshly cut head. He rubbed his temples, warding off the fury threatening to once again consume him.

"Listen to yourself Sheridan. Think about what just happened in there."

"I still can't believe this shit is happening." He leaned on the glass counter, staring at the only person in the world he could talk to about this bullshit. He wanted so much to throw something or beat someone. He felt so helpless and yet he had so much he needed to do now.

"I hear ya. The minute I saw him I knew. So he's Tariq's father?" Terrence sat down in one of the patio chairs, keeping his attention focused on the man standing at the bar.

"That's what the DNA test said. I can't believe he slept with my wife. I should have known, man. We didn't talk much about it but her friends confronted me some months ago talking about they saw me out with some other women." God, how could he have not seen this coming? His mother had even warned him that Winston had been asking about him lately.

"Winston too?" This was getting more fucked up by the minute. Sheridan had told him about the drama between him and his brother but Terrence never thought anyone would stoop so low to get back at his own flesh and blood.

"Probably." Sheridan just closed his eyes and shook his head. He was such a fool.

"Does Amira know?"

"I doubt it. They gave me the impression that they tried to tell her but she wasn't hearing it. She confronted me when she found a card from a hotel. Apparently Winston stayed there using my identity. But I was able to prove to her that I went on my trip so as far as I know, she was fine with it. Not only that, Amira knew I had a brother but she didn't know that we were twins. I guess this is as much my fault as it is his. If I'd have only told her maybe…"

"Don't go blaming yourself on this one. Winston knew what he was doing. You may be guilty of not telling Amira that you two were twins but it was all on him to manipulate the situation and take advantage. He's one hundred percent responsible for his actions."

"I guess you're right. It's still fucked up though. I should have believed her when she told me she hadn't done anything. She's never given me any indication that she'd step outside of our marriage for anything. I owe her such a big apology."

"I know Amira. She'll understand. It may take her some time but I'm sure you two can work this out. Now my question is who's going to break the news that a twin brother she didn't know about is Tariq's biological father?"

"Oh, don't worry about that one. He's going to tell her what he did." Sheridan walked from behind the bar making his way closer to the back door. He thrust his fist into his jacket pockets, still more than fuming. He had to be rational about this.

"And what about Tariq?" Terrence kept an eye on his boy, making sure that flicker of what he saw earlier didn't rear its head again. He was glad he'd decided to come down; otherwise he'd probably be on the way to the police station as a witness to a murder.

Sheridan took in a deep breath, holding it in for a moment before exhaling. "I can't say right now. I guess that's going to be up to Amira."

They turned as the door opened. Both men scowled at Winston as he intruded upon their conversation. He refused to waver at their scrutiny. He wanted to be a part of his son's life and neither Sheridan nor his friend was going to deny him that chance.

"Sheridan, I fucked up and I know that but I never meant..."

"Save it. Let's go. You're going to tell Amira what you did." Sheridan turned back to Terrance, prepared to offer some sort of restitution for the damage done to his house. Terrence stopped him before he could say the words.

"Don't worry about it man. And you can come back and get your stuff whenever. Tell Amira if she needs anything, don't hesitate to call."

Sheridan appreciated the support of his friend. He was more than sure he'd be leaning on Terrance a lot in the next coming weeks. He wasn't sure how this whole thing was going to pan out with his wife and the new baby but Sheridan vowed to stand by her side and support her in any decision she made.

This child was just as much a part of her as he was Winston. She'd carried him for nearly nine months, endured so many physical challenges trying to nurture this baby to term. She'd formed an immediate bond with him and if she wanted to keep this baby then he was more than willing to welcome him into the family.

DOUBLETAKE

Amira, Sheridan & Winston

Making sure to keep his brother within his sight, Sheridan stormed his way into the hospital to see his wife. He felt like such a fool for accusing her of knowingly cheating on him. Truth be told, he was just as responsible for this as Winston was. If he'd have told her about the twin situation, none of this might have happened. He stopped in front of the hospital room, peeking into the window only to see that the stacks of presents, wall of cards, piles of balloons and teddy bears were gone.

He stopped a nurse coming down the walkway in their direction. "Excuse me, can you tell me where my wife was moved."

The young woman looked up at the concerned face and then at the room number. "If you mean Mrs. Malcolm, she and the baby were discharged a few hours ago."

"Thanks." Sheridan glared at his brother. "They're probably at the house. Let's go." He waited for Winston to precede him down the narrow hallway.

The two men didn't say so much as a word to each other on the drive from the hospital to the house. Sheridan ignored his ringing cell phone, choosing to focus his attention on getting to his wife. So many pieces were falling into place. The questions from Carmen and Madison about seeing him out with other women, the accusations of cheating, Sheridan would bet top dollar that it was Winston they'd seen at that hotel that night. Even Nasir had been partially correct when he thought he saw his father the night Amira had taken the pills. Winston must have somehow gotten into the house and Nasir must have caught him before he could leave.

Sheridan's anger grew the more he thought about Winston in his bed, defiling his wife's body without her knowledge. God. If he had only stayed home, she wouldn't have taken those pills. But would she have been able to tell the difference between them even if she hadn't?

Sheridan pulled into the driveway, his grip so tight on the steering wheel his knuckles were beginning to turn white. Why? Why after all of these years would his brother come back into his life only to ruin it? He'd ask the question once he made sure Amira was all right.

"You sure this is a good idea?" Winston stared up at the home he'd ruined. Amira didn't deserve what he'd done to her. He never should have taken his revenge at Sheridan out on that poor, innocent woman.

"Shut the fuck up. You don't have a say in this. You did this and for once in your life, you're going to face the consequences of your actions. Now get out." Sheridan sat back, waiting for this punk to climb out of his vehicle.

He expected Winston to try to weasel his way out of this the same way he weaseled his way out of everything else since they were children. Not this time. Sheridan had had it. For once, he was glad his brother had stayed out of his life. Too bad things couldn't have just remained that way.

With his brother standing at the front of the truck and his eyes still fixed on the decorative front door, Sheridan climb out. He nearly snarled at Winston as he walked up the stairs and unlocked the door. He glanced over his shoulder, wondering when his brother was going to chicken out but when the face so much like his own stayed one step behind him, he swung the door open and entered the quiet house.

Sheridan walked down the narrow hallway, tossing his keys on the table by the door before entering the living room. Three sets of eyes turned in his direction. Tara, Carmen, and Madison sat on the couch, gawking at him, waiting for him to say something, anything.

Tara narrowed her gaze, a clear indication of the anger she harbored at her soon to be ex-brother-in-law. How dare he call Amira the names he'd called her and leave her in that hospital with a newborn baby?

All three women gave him a curious glance as they heard the front door slam, indicating that there was someone with him. The three sets of eyes grew wide and darted between him and what he was sure was his twin brother. He hadn't turned around to see if Winston was standing there but, based upon the reaction of the women, he was more than sure his brother was behind him.

He pointed at the chair across from the women, silently ordering his brother to take a seat. Normally Winston didn't take kindly to orders, however, under the circumstances, after what he'd done and the beating Sheridan had given him at his boy's house, he didn't want to push any more buttons. It was time for him to be a man and fess up to his mistakes and his responsibilities.

"Can I talk to you," Sheridan's eyes darted from Carmen to Madison. His gaze finally came to rest on Tara, "in private."

He didn't wait for her to respond. Instead, he walked behind the couch into the kitchen, away from prying eyes and ears. Sheridan stood in front of the small window, his fingers wrapped around the edge of the counter and the sink. This was probably the hardest thing he'd ever had to do.

Tara kept her distance, pulling up the swinging door between the kitchen and the dining room, giving them a little more privacy. She slid a chair from beneath the kitchen table and took a seat. Her eyes fixed on her brother-in-law her mind still tried to process what she'd just seen.

"You know, he hasn't said so much as one word to me in seventeen years." Sheridan lowered his head, hating himself for not telling them the whole truth about Winston from the start.

"Why Sheridan? Why didn't you tell Amira that you and your brother were twins?" Tara tried to keep her cool about this but she was still angry that Sheridan had kept this secret.

"I don't have a brother. I haven't had a brother in a long time, since way before she and I met. He made sure of that." He closed his eyes and shook his head. This was so fucked up, especially since he'd only recently been considering trying to get back in touch with his brother and, somehow working things out so that his children would know their uncle. Now that would never happen.

"So is he…" Tara's words trailed off.

Sheridan understood her question. Unfortunately, she already knew the answer. He'd only confirm it. "He said she didn't know. That night she took the pills…"

"So Nasir did see someone that night, except it wasn't you, it was your brother." She cut him off watching the pain talking about this was causing him. The only reason she was asking was because her sister was back in the bedroom suffering because of lack of information and, in the end, she'd probably have to help her put the pieces of her life back together.

"I never thought Winston would stoop this low; and I've seen him do some trifling shit in our lifetime." Sheridan turned his head to look Tara in the face when he asked his next question. "How is she?"

It was Tara's turn to look away. She lowered her head, busying her fingers twirling a paper napkin around them until she wound it between each one. "Not good. Not good at all. She won't take care of the baby. She's been in the bedroom since we got home from the hospital. I finally had to take Tariq in the nursery. I was actually afraid she might hurt him."

Sheridan doubled over as some unknown pain shot through him. It felt like someone had stabbed him in the chest with a knife and now they were twisting it around while pouring salt in the wound. He didn't know how they were going to get through this but somehow they'd figure things out. Now that he knew the truth, he needed to apologize to Amira and try to make things right.

Sheridan couldn't blame her. Winston had raped her, taking something from her while she lay helpless, her mind trapped in some intoxicated slumber. He pushed the thoughts out of his mind. Focusing that anger and manipulating it into something else, Sheridan drew in a deep breath and slowly released it out through his mouth.

"I brought him here to tell her. If he was man enough to do what he did, he should be man enough to tell her to her face."

"Sheridan, I don't know if that's such a good idea."

"Now you sound like him."

"Look, don't you think she's been through enough? Normally, I'd agree but she's in a real fragile state. She's still trying to even figure out when all of this happened. She still doesn't believe that Tariq isn't your child."

"But that's because she's looking at him. The test didn't lie. Neither Amira nor I carry the sickle cell trait, Winston does. My blood type is O; Winston is AB that would explain how Tariq ended up with an AB blood type. And though I still haven't figured out how he pulled it off, he had a DNA test run. Tariq is his son."

"I don't know what to tell you. But before you drop this in her lap, I think you need to talk to her first. After that, if you think she can handle this, then I'd say make him tell her. But just know there is going to be some backlash and with Amira, I can't tell you for sure how it's going to come out."

Tara slid her chair from beneath the table and prepared to check on the kids.

"Tara, wait."

She stopped, her arm outstretched, ready to push the

door open. She chose to not turn around. Instead, she listened for the words Sheridan wanted to say to her.

"Thanks for being there for her. I've been an ass and I don't know what I am going to have to do to make this up to Amira but I want you to know I'm standing by her one hundred percent on this. I love her. And I always will."

"Make sure you tell her that. Right now she really needs to hear it." Tara stepped out the door, leaving Sheridan to get himself together before he faced his wife. She just hoped her sister would be able to get past this.

DOUBLETAKE

Sheridan and Amira

S heridan stood in front of the bedroom door listening for any sign of Amira on the other side. Only silence emanated from behind the closed door. To his surprise, only silence came from the living room as well. He wondered what kind of questions Amira's friends were asking Winston. He wondered if they'd figured out it was Winston they'd seen with those other women and not him.

Sheridan's hand hovered above the doorknob. He still hadn't figured out what he was going to say to her. And even if he had, he wasn't sure she'd believe him. That's one reason he'd brought Winston to the house. He didn't want to cause Amira any additional stress, especially after she'd just given birth but this was his only chance to try to make this right and the sooner this was over, the sooner his brother would be out of his life. Permanently.

Sheridan rested his head against the door praying for the strength to face Amira after walking out on her the way he had. If she forgave him for this, he promised to honor her everyday in any and every way he could think of. She was his queen, always had been and always would be. Tired, anxious, and a little hopeful, he turned the knob and entered the room. He closed the door quietly behind him not wanting anyone to hear the hopeful reconciliation between him and his wife. As he leaned on the door he heard Amira's sniffling echoed in the enclosed space. He never meant for her to cry. He hadn't meant to cause her any distress and yet, he'd done that and more. He'd broken her heart.

Sheridan trudged his way across the sitting room into the bedroom he hadn't seen in a couple of days. He expected to find Amira curled up in the bed. But she wasn't there. He searched, listening, as the sniffles grew louder. He followed the whimpers and gasps, finding her rolled up in a ball on the floor between the wall and his side of the bed. She'd wrapped her arms around his pillow and buried her face in it. Kneeling beside her he placed a hand on her bare arms.

Amira turned teary eyes up at the man who'd intruded upon her misery. "Just take your stuff and go," she somehow managed, trying her best to keep the sob deep within from escaping.

"I'm not leaving." He slid a finger beneath her chin gazing down into her eyes. They were tired, puffy. She'd probably been crying since he'd left her in the hospital. What should be a joyous time for her had turned into a time of mourning.

"Why are you doing this? Why are you torturing me? I'm not giving up my babies Sheridan; they're all I have." She pleaded with him to just let her be. She really couldn't do this right now. She was on the verge of a breakdown and she couldn't deal with him too.

"I'm not taking them away baby. If anything I'm hoping for your forgiveness." He offered her a hand praying she'd at least give him a chance to explain. He'd done her so wrong and only a miracle could get them through this.

Sheridan's tension eased as she slid her fingers into his. He pulled her into a warm embrace, holding on to her as if it were their last day together. He feared it might be but he was more than prepared to face whatever questions she mighty have. He still held some of the responsibility for this but something inside told him she'd forgive him for keeping the secret.

Scooping her into his arms Sheridan laid Amira on the bed. He slid in behind her positioning them so that she sat between his legs with her back resting against his chest. He wrapped his arms around her, holding her close to his heart. He needed to feel her in his arms, some sort of reassurance that somehow he'd be able to fix this.

Amira continued to cry, not knowing why all of a sudden her husband had decided to come back. She wanted to tell him how sorry she was but she was still grappling with the fact that Tariq wasn't his son. None of this made sense. The only thing she could think of was that someone had broken into the house the night Nasir said he saw his daddy, the night she'd mixed medicine and alcohol. She'd endangered her children and she felt like the worse mother in the world.

Still, even that didn't explain how it was that Tariq looked just like Sheridan. If someone had raped her while she was out, why, how could that baby look so much like her other children, so much like Sheridan.

"I will love you and Tariq for all eternity," Sheridan whispered the words to his wife, hoping in some way they'd comfort her. He squeezed the trembling body held securely in his arms wanting so much to make her pain go away.

"I know the truth baby and this wasn't your fault." When she started to speak, Sheridan hushed the delicate flower in his arms. "Please, let me speak my peace."

When she quieted down, intertwining her fingers with his, he understood that she'd allow him to get whatever he held inside off of his chest.

"There is so much I should have told you; so much you should still know. Part of this is my fault." Sheridan laid his head on the maple veneer headboard of their king sized bed. Taking in a breath and releasing it through his mouth, he revealed the one thing he'd hidden from his wife for a long time. "Amira, baby, I never meant for any of this to happen. I never thought my own flesh and blood would stoop so low. I know who Tariq's father is."

"Who?" Amira pulled from his grasp. She turned around; the need to look him in the eyes when he revealed who Tariq's father was drove every move.

"There's one thing that I never told you about my brother. He and I are twins."

Amira just stared at him with a blank expression. He felt her retreat to that place in her mind where nothing and everything made sense. He understood that she needed to process the words he'd just said. She was a smart woman; she'd figure out what it was he was trying to tell her. At least that is what he hoped. She grew limp, her body falling forward as emotion overwhelmed her. Sheridan just held on as she cried and rocked and poured all of the hurt and anger and confusion out. She still didn't grasp the full effect of what he was telling her.

Sheridan couldn't fight back his tears anymore. His eyes traced the room, his imagination running wild. His mind formed glimpses of the events of the night his brother had intruded upon his humble abode. His anger flared with each wail his wife released. He cried with her, sharing in the anguish but not being able to relate to the full spectrum of emotion he was sure she was attempting to cope with.

"Why, Sheridan?" Amira beat her fist into her husband's chest as another bout of anger flowed from within. "Why would he do this to me?"

"I honestly don't know. But he has something to say to you. He's here." Sheridan waited for some sort of reaction.

She backed away but he refused to allow her to put too much space between them. The color drained from her face as she gave in and allowed him to pull her back to him. Amira crawled into her husband's arms, still not completely understanding why or how any of this happened. She'd never seen Winston. Sheridan had only mentioned his name once, when it had slipped out about the fact that he even had a brother. Since that day, whenever she brought it up, he shut her down.

Was that what the last few months of his escapades in the sitting room were about? Had he been in there wondering where his brother was? Maybe that's why he'd made sure whenever his mother called that he left the room.

"Amira, I'm so sorry this happened." Sheridan didn't know what else to say.

"What does he want?" The anguish, hurt and sadness had turned to anger. Anger was something she could feed from. Anger was something she could hold on to and right now that was exactly what Amira needed.

"For once in his life, to tell the truth." Sheridan held the quivering woman close to his heart. She was strong. He just wondered if she was strong enough to make it through this.

"Baby?"

"I don't think I can do this Sheridan. I can't do this." Just as quickly as it had come, her anger dissipated.

"Sure you can, baby." Something inside convinced Sheridan that this would be therapeutic for Amira. If she wanted to get through this, she'd have to face the person responsible for almost tearing their family apart.

"No! I can't. Why did he come here? Hasn't he done enough?" She wiped the tears from her eyes, staring up into the face she'd missed so much. She didn't want to hear the truth. She wanted Tariq to be Sheridan's son.

"You deserve his apology Amira. You deserve to have him look you in the face and admit that he was more than wrong. He owes you that much and so much more."

Seeing the love in Sheridan's eyes, she knew this wasn't just about her. His brother needed to pay and the best way to make him do that was by making him grovel at her feet, beg for her forgiveness for what he did to her and to her family. Not wanting to disappoint her man, Amira searched within for the strength to do this. Somehow she'd gather up enough nerve to pull herself together and face this sorry excuse for a man.

They'd figure the rest of this out later. In the meantime, she wanted to get this over with. She had a few choice words for Winston once she came face to face with him. She intertwined her fingers with Sheridan's, looking up into his eyes.

"Give me a second to get cleaned up and we'll do this together."

Instead of letting her go, Sheridan pulled his wife closer. "I meant what I said Amira. I don't care what the DNA test said, I don't give a damn about DNA tests. All I care about is you and my family. Tariq is my family and I will love you both for as long as I live."

No longer able to deny the desire rushing through his body, Sheridan did what he'd been dying to do since he found out what his brother had done. He kissed Amira liked he'd never kissed her before, and as his lips melded with hers, he reaffirmed his love for the only woman who'd been able to truly capture his heart.

DOUBLETAKE

Amira, Sheridan & Winston

With her fingers intertwined with her husband's, Amira walked only a half a step behind Sheridan as they exited the bedroom. Normally they walked side by side, but she was feeling a little intimidated by all of this. It was one thing to meet her husband's twin brother but it was another to be faced with that same stranger, knowing that he'd crept into her bedroom, had sex with her while she lay unconscious, touched her children all while pretending to be her husband.

Sheridan stopped before they rounded the corner. He wrapped his hands around hers, looking down into her beautiful brown eyes. He saw fear in them and sadness. He watched hurt run beneath her loving eyes. He almost wanted to not do this, to just tell Winston to get the hell out of their lives and never look back. Under the circumstances though, that wasn't an option. He'd crossed the line in so many ways and Amira deserved better.

"You know I love you baby, don't you?"

Amira only nodded. She saved her thoughts but took

comfort in the fact that she still had her family and she wasn't being blamed for this situation with Tariq. She wasn't fooling herself; there was still so much they needed to discuss but she held hope now, something she'd almost given up on when Sheridan had walked out on her in the hospital.

"You ready for this?"

She didn't want to talk anymore so she pulled him toward the corner but stopped before rounding it. She'd allow her husband, as head of household, the honor of being the first to enter the room full of people she was sure were waiting for them.

With a newfound confidence, Sheridan stepped into the open area of the living room with Amira appearing behind him. He pulled her closer, indicating that she should stand by his side as his equal.

In a rugged voice clearly laced with anger, Sheridan addressed the people sitting in the room. "If you're not family, get out." He wasn't going to be nice about this. The time for nice went out of the door the minute Winston invaded this once happy home.

Sheridan eyed Carmen and Madison, waiting for them to gather their things to leave. The two women one by one approached, giving Amira a hug and telling her that if she needed them, all she had to do was pick up the phone. She smiled at her friends still holding on to her silence.

No one said a word as the two women who obviously didn't like being kept out of the loop sashayed down the hall. Sheridan waited until he heard the front door close before leading Amira past the chair where his brother sat and helped her sit on the couch next to her sister. He took a seat on the other side of his wife, holding her hand as she stared at the man in the chair with his head hung low.

Amira turned worried eyes up at her husband as some unsettling feelings began to emerge. She'd convinced herself that she could do it, but now, seeing Winston, knowing what he'd done, she wasn't so sure.

"It's okay Amira, I know this is hard. But you're strong." He squeezed her hand, sharing his strength with her. He looked over at his brother before speaking. "Look at her."

Winston raised his head and for the first time in the light he laid eyes on the woman whose life he'd just altered. He couldn't really say he'd ruined her life. From what he could tell, she still had Sheridan and apparently she was okay with the baby.

"Well, don't you have something to say?" Sheridan wasn't playing with Winston. He was here to apologize so he needed to get to kissing Amira's ass.

"Amira…"

"Uh, that's Mrs. Malcolm to you." Sheridan wasn't going to tolerate an ounce of disrespect from his brother. Maybe if he'd gone about things the right way he'd have earned the right to call Amira by her first name.

"Point taken." Winston's eyes darted over at his brother before he turned his gaze back to his sister-in-law. "Mrs. Malcolm I owe you more than just an apology for the wrong I've done. When I first came down to Atlanta, I came with the hopes of making things right with my brother."

Sheridan covered Amira's hand; stopping the words

she was about to say. He wanted the apology before anything. He knew if Amira started, Winston would never get the words out so he hoped she understood his reason for quieting her.

"I don't know how much of our past Sheridan has told you…"

"Get on with it Winston, she doesn't need to hear the drama story of our past." More than irritated, Sheridan's foot started to tap and he tightened his fingers around Amira's. She placed her other hand on top of his, calming his nerves with a gentle touch.

"I'm sorry, Mrs. Malcolm. I'm sorry for sneaking into your home while you slept. I'm sorry for any stress I may have caused you. I'm sorry for using you to get back at my brother. But most of all, I'm sorry that I violated you. I never intended for any of this to happen. I never meant to cause you any harm and I never meant to leave you here with a child you thought was Sheridan's."

That was it. Amira had held on, convincing herself that once this was all over, they could go back to their happy little lives. But now everything was sinking in: the stories that Madison and Carmen had told her, Nasir swearing to her that Sheridan had been in the house. And then there was the baby; that precious little boy in the nursery, the little boy who'd wreaked havoc on her system during pregnancy; that little boy who she didn't know if she could love. It was him all along.

Amira felt the first set of tears fall. Then the faucets from her eyes opened to full flow. She broke down. Falling over into her husband's arms, she wailed as the anguish took over. Her baby, her precious innocent baby, was a product of this monster. Crying like she'd never cried before, Amira pulled away from Sheridan. She stood, walking over to where Winston sat. Balling up her fist, she punched Winston as hard as she could before running down the hallway and slamming the bedroom door so hard the walls rattled.

Hearing the sound of Tariq crying, Tara stood and made her way down the opposite wing of the house toward the nursery. Sheridan remained on the couch, pinching the bridge of his nose, warding off a rage-induced headache. He glanced in his brother's direction, watching as Winston wiped the blood from his nose. Sheridan didn't know Amira had it in her. He'd never seen her raise a finger to kill a poor senseless spider much less gather enough strength to punch a man hard enough to cause him to bleed.

"Don't go anywhere, this isn't over." Sheridan left his trifling brother sitting alone in the living room. He knew Winston wouldn't leave. He figured his brother still had it in his head that he'd get to be a part of Tariq's life. As far as Sheridan was concerned, the polar caps would no longer exist before Winston ever so much as laid an eye on that little boy.

"Amira!" Sheridan called to her first, hoping to coax her to open the door. When he received no response and he didn't hear anything he tried the door. Locked. "Amira!" he banged harder now panic setting in. "Amira, open the door please!"

Bad thoughts started running through his head, thoughts of her hurting herself. Maybe Tara had been right. Maybe this hadn't been such a good idea. He stepped back, prepared to take the risk of her being behind the door when he broke it down. Just as he was about to knock the door down, a hand on his shoulder stopped him.

"Let me try." Tara stepped around Sheridan, getting as close to the door as she possibly could. "Amira. Amira, its Tara. Open the door." She listened for any sound but heard nothing.

"We have to get to her, Tara. She might hurt herself."

Tara turned, placing a finger over her lips. When Sheridan quieted, down she again turned to the door and spoke, "When all seems lost, Mother Earth will replenish us. When the heavens appear empty, look a moment longer and you shall see the flicker of life reveal itself to you," Tara knelt, sliding something Sheridan couldn't see beneath the door, "warming your heart, freeing you from all negative energy." The lock on the door turned and the door opened slightly. As Tara continued the prayer she and her sister had written many years ago while visiting a Choctaw reservation, Amira spoke the words with her, "When your spirit begins to fade and your energy returns to Mother Earth, rejoice because you have given back that which you have taken and once again completed the circle."

Tara slipped through the opening of the door, pushing it closed behind her. Sheridan stared at the closed door wondering if Tara would really be able to help her sister. Praying that she could, he turned. He had one last score to settle with his brother and there was no better time than the present.

Sheridan and Winston

The air in the living room was thicker than molasses. Sheridan hadn't said as much as two words to Winston since he'd left Tara and Amira to try to work things out. He'd hoped to hear something, anything, but the longer he paced, the more the feeling of hopelessness took up residence within.

"Look, I need to go handle some things."

Sheridan stopped at the sound of his brother's voice. What could he possible have to handle. All he'd ever done was manipulate people into believing that he was a good guy. Well, his little world of make believe, as far as Sheridan was concerned, was long gone.

"Explain this to me." Sheridan chose not to comment on the I need to go handle some business speech, "Why Winston. Why after all of this time would you come back and do this?"

"You still haven't figured it out, have you?" Winston

stood and made his way over to the window. Staring out into the now darkening sky, he finally realized that in all of these years, Sheridan had never figured out why he'd left.

"Haven't figure out what? You? I don't think I'll ever figure you out."

"That's not what I'm talking about." Winston placed his hands behind his back. He still faced the window but he spoke loud enough for his brother to hear him. "I loved her, you know."

"Who? What are you talking about Winston?" Now his brother was talking crazy. The longer he looked at the man, the more convinced he became that Winston had lost all sense of right and wrong.

"Bianca. I loved her."

"What does she have to do with this?"

Winston whipped around, staring his brother down like the school bully. "You stole her from me."

"What the fuck are you talking about? I never even looked at Bianca." Where had that come from? Bianca had been far from his type. He'd assured Winston that he'd never date her and yet here his brother was accusing him of doing just that.

"Oh really? Then why were you two all hugged up on the couch?"

Hugged up on the couch? Sheridan thought back to their high school days around the last time he'd talked to his brother. He remembered that day; it was the same day Bianca came to the house looking for Winston. He'd thought he heard the front door close that day.

"What do you think was going on that day, Winston?"

"I know what I saw. You and her sitting on the couch with her face all buried in your chest, your arms all wrapped around her." It was Winston's turn to be angry. Sheridan had been the first to break the pact, or at least as far as he was concerned.

All this time. Sheridan started walking his little path behind the couch again. All this time over some bullshit his brother thought he saw.

"Don't try to deny it, Sheridan."

"I have nothing to deny. Unlike you I know the whole situation." Sheridan capped his anger. Him blowing up was the last thing Amira needed right now.

"What situation?" Curiosity quickly replaced Winston's anger. Had Jasmine been right all along? Had there really been something else going on that he didn't know about?

"Did you check your pager that day?"

"I don't know. That was fuckin' seventeen years ago."

"Then let me answer the question for you. No, you didn't check your pager that day. You didn't answer your cell phone either."

"So?" Winston walked closer to the chair he'd been sitting in only moments earlier.

"Sooo, if you had done either of those things, you would have known the truth." Sheridan stopped, looking his brother square in the eyes. He waited for the man to ask the question dangling on the tip of his tongue.

"Truth about what?"

"Bianca came to the house looking for yo ass. She needed you that night but as usual yo punk ass was out running the streets. Her best friend got killed that day."

Winston's legs gave way, sending his body plummeting into the chair. This whole thing had happened because he hadn't been there for his girl and he hadn't taken the time to find out all of the details before assuming. Guess his mother had been right about assuming.

Winston felt like such a fool. Now he'd lost the only chance to have his brother back in his life and all over some bullshit assumption. Had he have stuck around or even confronted them, he might sill have his girl and his brother.

"So what now?" Winston needed to know where this left them. If Sheridan wanted to fight over his son, then he was ready for the long haul.

"Now, you get the fuck out of my house and stay the hell away from my family." Sheridan glared at the man with his head hung low. If his brother so much as thought he was going to be a part of Tariq's life, he was sadly mistaken.

"And what about my son?"

"Get the fuck out, Winston." His expression said it all. Winston was treading in deep shark infested water.

Winston stood, realizing that his brother was in far from a rational mind. He decided it was best to leave this be for now. He planned to do what he had to do to see his son even if it tore his family apart even more.

Sheridan

Sheridan leaned against the door in the master bedroom watching his wife stare out into space. He'd only left her side a few hours a day in the last week, mostly to talk with his lawyers about pressing charges against his brother and to protect Tariq's interest. He and Amira had talked at length about whether she wanted to press charges and she assured her husband that she did so he'd called his lawyer that day and they'd started the procedures for filing criminal charges.

Sheridan couldn't stand to see his wife like this. She should be happy, enjoying bonding with the baby. Instead, she spent most of her time staring out into the back yard. She'd force herself to breast feed Tariq and as soon as he was done, she'd hand him off to Sheridan.

Things had gotten so bad that Amira couldn't even bathe alone. Sheridan had started to notice that she winced every time she sat down or someone touched her. He'd soon discovered that she'd been rubbing herself raw in the shower. Since then, he drew a bath for her every night and he'd wash her from head to toe. He didn't mind taking care of her, but as each day passed, she slipped further and further into a deep depression.

No longer able to allow this to continue, Sheridan made a decision about how to handle this. Sure that she would be fine while he went to talk to Tara, Sheridan slipped out of the door and headed out to the guesthouse.

He knocked on the door, his eyes turning in the direction of the main house. He'd seen Tara and Terrence bring the kids out to the backyard for a little playtime earlier. Nasir was sitting on the back porch of the main house, his head buried in coloring books as his hand scribbled on the pages. Sheridan was more than sure that baby girl and their other son were propped in front of the television in the guesthouse with his sister-in-law and best friend.

Sheridan paused at the sound of the door opening.

"Everything okay?" Tara asked, wondering why Sheridan had left Amira's side.

"Yes and no. Is Terrence still here?" Sheridan observed the glow in Tara's eyes at the mention of Terrence's name. Sooner or later they'd get hitched. He was sure of it.

"Yeah, come on in." She stepped to the side to let her brother-in-law into the house.

"Actually, can you two meet me in the house? I need to talk to you two but I don't want to leave Amira alone for too long."

"You sure everything's okay?" Tara didn't like the sadness beneath Sheridan's eyes. He looked tired, worn down. He was worried about her sister; she was just as worried as he was, but she had someone to talk to about it. Sheridan, being the man who never showed weakness, just kept everything inside.

"It will be. I'll be in the house."

Sheridan walked away from Tara, not wanting her to see how much all of this was taking a toll on him. He stopped on the back porch to check on Nasir before entering the back door to wait for Tara and Terrence.

After peeking in on Amira, Sheridan sat on the couch watching a blank television screen. The longer this went on the more he questioned whether or not they'd be able to get through this. Amira needed help, so he'd called his mother and asked if any of her therapist friends could recommend someone his wife could talk to. She'd passed along some information and they'd set up an appointment.

This was going to be so hard for the both of them. He knew every time she looked at him, she saw Winston and thought about what he'd done to her. She wouldn't even sleep in the same bed with Sheridan. When he tried to hold, her she pulled away. He tried to let her fall asleep first, hoping to just hold her through the night, but the minute she realized he'd slipped into the bed, she crawled out. So, wanting her to be as comfortable as possible, Sheridan had resorted to sleeping on the couch or the chaise in their bedroom.

Sheridan ignored the pitter-patter of little feet and the laughter of his baby girl as Terrence and Tara brought the other kids back into the main house. He heard Tara corralling the kids into the back bedroom to watch cartoons while the grown folks handled business.

"You a'ight man?" Terrence asked, sitting in the chair next to Sheridan.

"You want the truth?" Sheridan glanced in the man's direction before turning his gaze back to the blank TV.

"Truth is always good."

"No."

Before he could elaborate, Tara entered the living room. She joined the two men, taking the seat across from Terrence and to the left of Sheridan.

"So what did you want to talk to us about?"

Sheridan rubbed his head; his hands coming to rest for a moment over his eyes before he laid his head back and focused on the ceiling fan.

"I need to ask you two for a favor." He waited for either of them to say something, but they both remained quiet. "I need to get Amira some help. I talked to my mother and there's a therapist close to where she lives who may be able to help 'Mira."

"What do you need from us?" Terrence asked, somewhat understanding where Sheridan might be going with this.

Tara watched as Terrence stared at Sheridan. She knew that whatever he needed for them to do, they'd be there to do it.

"Well, I need to take her to my folk's place so that she can talk to this therapist. I plan to take Tariq with us. But I was hoping that you two could watch the rest of the kids. We'll be gone about a week."

"Consider it done." Whether Terrence could be there or not, Tara would do what needed to be done to make sure her sister's family stayed together.

"We'll make sure the kids are taken care of. You just

make sure Amira and Tariq get what they need. Have you told Amira about your plans?" Though Terrence knew Amira considered Sheridan the decision maker of the family, since this very much concerned her, he wanted to make sure this wasn't going to cause any additional stress for his friend.

"Yeah. She said if you two agreed, then she'd go along with this. I know this has been hard for her. And the fact that my brother and I look just alike hasn't made this any easier. I see the way she looks at me sometimes. I know she's seeing him. I can only imagine what thoughts might be running through her head."

Tara got up from the chair and sat down next to Sheridan on the couch. She opened her arms to him and he allowed the woman to hug him.

"You're doing the right thing," she said to him. Her brother-in-law was so strong but Sheridan needed to deal with his feelings as well.

"Thanks Tara." Sheridan pulled out of her grasp. "And thank you too," he said to Terrence. "I don't know how we'd make it without you two."

Tara stood, "I'll help get Amira packed." She crossed the living room, heading down the hallway toward the master bedroom.

"You all right with this?" Terrence didn't want to push, but the last thing Amira needed right now was for Sheridan to blow up.

"Yeah. The funny thing is, things don't really feel that different. I mean, what Amira is going through and the problems that she and I are having, I expect. But I thought

I'd feel some sort of loss knowing that my brother was completely out of my life for good."

"So there's no chance for you two reconciling?" Terrence already knew the answer to the question but he was thinking about Tariq. Sooner or later, that little boy needed to know the truth about who his biological father was.

"It'll be a cold day in hell before that happens." Sheridan didn't want to talk about this anymore. Winston was out of his life for good and he was more than happy for things to remain that way.

"One more question and I'll drop it."

"What?" Sheridan eyed Terrence, wondering what was on the man's mind.

"Are you ever going to tell Tariq the truth? I mean if something happens and he gets sick…"

"When he's old enough to understand the entire situation we'll tell him." Sheridan pushed his weight up from the couch. "I'd better get packed."

"Don't worry about this, Sheridan. You and Amira are going to be just fine."

"I hope you're right man. I pray to God you're right." Sheridan turned the corner, walking towards the master bedroom. As much as he wanted to believe they'd be fine, only time would tell if Amira really could get past this and their family could get back to normal.

Epilogue

Sheridan wrapped his arm around his wife as they waited for the judge to return with a decision in the custody battle over Tariq. He still couldn't believe his brother had the nerve to even think he'd get custody of that little boy. Sheridan thought the time his brother spent in jail for raping Amira would be enough for him to get the picture.

He could only imagine the look on Winston's face when he was served with the warrant for his arrest. The entire trial, Winston glared at Sheridan and Amira in a pitiful attempt to spook him. But Sheridan held steadfast. Winston had admitted to both him and Terrence that he'd broken into the house and had sex with Amira while she was intoxicated and under the influence of the sleeping pills. The jury quickly sentenced him to eighteen months behind bars.

Sheridan just hoped that all of this would be over soon. Amira had finally started to open up and form a bond with Tariq. After the time she'd spent with her in-laws and her therapy sessions, she'd decided that her love for her husband and children would be enough to help her make it through this trying time. She still found sleeping with Sheridan in the same bed difficult sometimes but he'd assured her that he'd be by her side no matter what and he'd be as patient as she needed him to be.

Amira cradled Tariq in her arms. He was such a blessing. At least something beautiful had come out of this horrible situation. He was her light at the end of the tunnel. Every time he smiled at her or laughed, her heart warmed. He'd always be special to her, no matter what.

Sheridan helped Amira up as the bailiff instructed everyone to rise before the judge reentered the courtroom. He pulled her closer as they sat down. They cradled their son between them as the little boy wrapped his tiny fingers around the gold cross-hung from his mother's neck.

"After reviewing the facts in this case…"

The judge's voice trailed off as Sheridan felt Amira begin to shake in his arms. If the judge gave Winston custody of Tariq, all that his wife had put her trust in would be gone. Tariq had become her new rock. Nurturing him, helping him grow up into a good man had been what she'd turned to when everything else in life felt like it was out of her grasp. If that judge took her baby away, Sheridan knew that Amira would probably go mad.

"…I cannot in good conscious grant you custody of this child. Petition for custody denied."

Hearing the final words from the judge, the banging of the gavel solidifying the decision, Sheridan pulled his family into his arms. He rocked Amira as she cried in his arms. Their family would remain whole.

From the corner of his eye, Sheridan caught a glimpse

of his brother sitting at the table with his lawyer. His head hung down, his shoulder slumping forward. Winston had just lost the last ounce of family he had left. Sheridan felt bad that he didn't care, but in the end, Winston had made his own bed and now he'd spend the rest of his life lying in it.

With his son in his arms and his wife by his side, Sheridan walked away from the past with only bright hopes for the future. A future with his wife, four children, a sister-in-law, his best friend, his mother and father and a successful business and not a regret or a worry in the world. If they could make it through this, then they could take anything life dished out to them.

DOUBLETAKE

ABOUT THE AUTHOR

Ana'Gia Wright is a firm believer that reading and writing go hand and hand. A southerner through and through she loves her peaches and pecans while curling up with a good book. A master of resourcefulness her love of research leads her down paths of discovery that touch every aspect of her writing. Her love of reading ignited her passion for writing leading her to frequently fill page after page with tales of her beloved characters' adventures. An influence and an adversary she loves to sprinkle facts about her beloved Georgia throughout her fictional worlds. Sneak peeks of her projects, including those by her alter ego Aziza Sphinx, are always available on her website www.authoranagiawright.com.

Ana'Gia Wright is available for signings and book club discussions. Please feel free to contact her at 678-224-1065

or

anagia@authoranagiawright.com.

A SPECIAL THANK YOU TO XL IMAGES

www.ingramcontent.com/pod-product-compliance
Lightning Source LLC
Chambersburg PA
CBHW071300170626
46809CB00001B/295